THE INHABITANT OF

Alexis O'Riley

D1560308

HOLLY VANDYNE

First paperback edition August 2021

ISBN: 9798452608073

www.hollyvandyne.com

Dedication

To my dad, *my* twin, who encouraged me to be a writer and taught me to never give up.

1

The Mouth Eats a Poisoned Sandwich

Someone tried to kill me with a sandwich today.

Mom thinks I'm crazy. Overreacting. She thinks I put too much sugar in my Kool-Aid or something stupid like that.

But she's wrong. My mom is always wrong.

Exhibit one. She said I'd be invited to Cole Mariano's birthday party this year. *She was on the PTO with his mom now! It was a sure thing!* Only the party was three weeks ago and not only did my postal or verbal invitation never arrive, but I got a prank phone call at 11:37 pm that night from his house. They asked when I go back home to Ireland if I would bring them back a magically delicious

5

pot of gold. I guess if the body they give your brain has red hair, green eyes, and freckles, that means you have to be Irish. I was pretty proud of myself – I didn't cry until I hung up.

Exhibit two. Last week she said the car had enough gas to get me to Dr. Hursh's for my 2:15 appointment. Wrong. I had to roast in the passenger seat of Mom's stalled Volvo in a pet store parking lot while she walked to the nearest gas station. This body walked through the glass door with "Dr. Hursh, Neurosurgeon" in small, neat white letters at exactly 3:07. He still saw me since I was his 'special' case, but I felt bad for making the eight pairs of tired, bored eyes in the waiting room wait longer.

Exhibit three. She told me I'd get used to this body with its bright white skin, slow legs and annoying peanut allergy. But it's been a year and I still hate every freckle and tangled red hair on it.

That's my mom – queen of all things wrong.

Just like the sandwich.

Before the accident, I ate peanut butter for breakfast. Big, heaping spoons of it. Chunky was my favorite, the more peanut chunks on the spoon, the better. But then I woke up in a new body. Now, one peanut, even a trace of it in any kind of food, will kill me. How's that for luck?

"No peanuts," I told the thin old woman with the hairnet staring at me from behind the metal counter. It was obvious that she was confused.

"Sea shunts?"

I had no idea what that was. The kid next to me giggled.

"PEA-NUTS," I repeated louder, clearer. "Can't eat them. I'm allergic."

"Ah, yeah, well you don't have to worry, sweetie. The district won't let us keep a peanut within a hundred miles of here." I nodded. I already knew the answer. But Mom still makes me tell them. Every. Single. Day. And I'm pretty sure half of the students here are on her payroll to spy on me and make sure I do what I'm 'supposed' to do.

I took the first bite of ham sandwich and glanced to where Cole sat at the far end of the cafeteria. Would it have been so hard for him to invite me to that party? Apparently so. I waited for him to look my way with hope that I'd see some guilt on his face, but he never turned. No one ever looks my way unless they need someone to tease.

Suddenly I couldn't breathe. The room spun. I fell from the bench, my brain frozen. I had no idea what was happening, and no clue what to do about it. Luckily, the right hand had a mind of its own. It reached into my bag and grabbed the EpiPen.

The hand held it out in front of me as I sucked in the small amount of air I was still able to inhale. I looked at the huge pen in horror.

No, no, NO! I hate shots!

I didn't know how to use it. Well, technically, I suppose I did, no one will give you an EpiPen without showing you how to use it. I vaguely remember punching the pen into an orange and thinking if I ever had to do that to my thigh, I'd pass out before the needle ever made it in. But my brain was in shock and any instructions I may have gotten left my head along with the ability to breathe.

The right hand knew exactly how to open the pen. It flipped the top, swung the arm and jabbed it into the thigh through my jeans. The mouth opened for a scream when it clicked and pricked and a sharp pain shot through the leg, but the scream came out silent. There was no air left for it.

The pen did what it needed to do. The throat opened and once I got more air, I calmed down a little. People I hadn't noticed before crowded around me. I smiled and laughed like an idiot; my natural defense mechanism against embarrassment. A few of them laughed nervously back. But none of them offered to help or asked if I was going to be okay.

Would I be okay? What does epinephrine do to you once it hits your bloodstream? The guy that made me murder the orange never told me that. Would my leg turn purple and fall off or would I bark like a dog?

Panic started to set in that the kids hovering around would call me Fido, so I scanned the crowd. Seeing Cole might distract me and take away any urge to lick my hand or wag my butt. But there was no blond haired, brown eyed knight in shining armor by the name of Cole to save me.

When the body could stand, I took it straight to the office and called Mom, who rushed to school and took me to the ER just to make sure I'd live.

* * *

Now I sit on a paper-covered bed, and wish I was anywhere on Earth but here in the emergency room.

Doctor Elizabeth Shayers wears leopard-spotted high heels and asks me to call her 'Liz', before she tells me I'm the healthiest fourteen-year-old she's seen in a long time and I can leave as soon as she signs off on the paperwork. Her long, curly brown hair keeps falling down from

9

her shoulders and covers the paper where she's trying to write. She stops mid-signature to pull it behind her head again. I'd give her a rubber band if I had one. If this is the beginning of her shift, she's going to need to tie that mess back.

"So your name is what again?" Dr. Shayers asks. Her eyes remind me of a cats. They're green and narrow and make her look like she's trying to figure something out. Like how I got poisoned by a sandwich.

"Vanessa Meadows. You're holding my chart, isn't it right there if you look down?" I feel a sharp jab behind the right arm where Mom stabs it with her fingernail. Her not-so-subtle way of telling me I'm being rude.

I try to wriggle the somewhat loose hospital band off of the wrist as she flips her hair back one last time.

"Well, Vanessa Meadows," She says my name slow like it's a snail making its way off of her tongue instead of words. "Your test results are back and there's not a trace of any nut in your system."

"She's lying," I say as soon as Dr. Shayer's hospital-inappropriate shoes click back down the hallway.

"Why would she do that, Vanessa?" I know when Mom's upset with me. She says my full name and splits it in two. The 'va' comes out in a higher tone like it's my first name, then the 'nessa' in a tone so low it could hit the floor. She fiddles with the channel button on the tiny TV attached to a swivel arm that swings wherever you want it to go. I don't care which way it goes and don't know why she's messing with it. I don't plan to stay here long enough to watch anything. I just want to go home.

"I don't know. Maybe she doesn't like me. Maybe the tests were wrong. Maybe the computer flaked when it was printing the results. Maybe she's not a real doctor. Did you see those shoes? No one in a hospital should be allowed to wear heels that could kill someone in a back alley."

Now, it's common knowledge that after my brain got transplanted into the stranger's body I became a hypochondriac. I get a splinter and am sure I'm facing impending death. So far I've been wrong. Maybe I'm more like my mom than I thought.

"Listen to how silly you sound. I just hope I don't lose my job for rushing out so fast. I didn't even have a chance to tell my boss; had to leave her a message. Speaking of messages, remind me to call Dr. Hursh's office when we get home so I can make him aware that we were here today."

"Why would you have to do that?" I argue. "He only cares about my brain. He's not going to care that someone tried to poison me with a sandwich."

"Va-nessa! Would you *please* stop saying that. No one tried to poison you with anything." She flips the switches on the TV faster, making me think it's a nervous tic or something. She can't possibly see what's on the screen before she hits the next channel button again. Obviously nothing I say about the sandwich is going to convince her, so I stop wasting my breath.

"I just want to be home, in my own bed, with my own TV that doesn't dangle perilously from an unstable plastic pipe. That's all."

She rolls her eyes. She doesn't think the eyes saw it, but they did. She can't possibly think I *like* feeling like a crazy person. In one single day my dad died and I was left with only the thoughts and memories stored in my brain. I never want to go through that again. Never, ever, never, never. Maybe I'm too careful now, but I'd rather be that than dead.

"You wear me out, Nessa." She sighs quietly. Her face shows the proof - dark circles surround her bloodshot eyes.

The truth is I wear myself out, too. It's not fun thinking I'm going to die every time I get a headache, pee a shade darker, or have a pinky finger twitch. All that's happened, and a ton more. And here I am. Still alive.

But this time I'm not being a hypochondriac. Someone really did try to poison me with a sandwich and no Mom or dangerous-heel-wearing doctor can convince me otherwise.

* * *

I stare at the stars that cover my bedroom ceiling. They're not glowing yet so they're hard to see and I have to strain the eyes. The days are longer now that spring's here and there's still too much light coming in through my bedroom window. Enough to keep me awake when I don't want to be.

And my brain won't shut down. Maybe because it's the only part of the original 'me' that's left. Tonight it makes me worry about peanuts. And it makes me miss my dad who was always the anti-Mom. When she was nervous, he calmed her down. When she was mad, he made her happy. As much as I've tried this past year, I'm just not able to do it like he could.

A sharp pain pierces the chest for a second and instantly the pores covering the skin drain sweat. Something's wrong. I'm going to die. I try to convince myself it's just a bubble of gas stuck in the body, floating around trying its hardest to make its way out and be free.

I never wanted to live like this. Unfortunately, I didn't have a choice.

My sad story is actually pretty simple.

The last thing I remember before the car accident was the time on the dashboard clock the same minute it happened. *1:34.* I was looking at it as a semi-truck crossed the double yellow line and hit the left side of our car head-on. Dad was driving. I was behind him. Mom, on the passenger side, wasn't hurt. It still amazes me that an accident that bad can kill one person and not touch another. They were sitting right next to each other.

My body was severely crushed from the chest down. But somehow I was still alive. Doctors took my brain and transplanted it into another girl's body. Dr. Hursh said she was brain-dead. Well, until she got mine.

"Do you believe in kismet, Nessa?" he asked when I finally woke after the surgeries.

He said it meant fate. Kismet that our bodies were a match and happened to be at the same hospital at the same time. They've been doing successful brain transplants for about five years now and while I wasn't the first, I was the youngest. He told me I should be proud of that but I'm not.

Now, lying in bed staring up at fake stars that don't light up nearly as bright as the real ones, I realize that I've been kidding myself. I did have a choice. If I would've just sat behind Mom, I still wouldn't have my dad but I might still have my body. It's sad how such a stupid little decision can change your life forever.

So sad that this body finally falls asleep covered in tears.

2

The Teeth Get Jealous

The metal bleachers are freezing this morning. The cold passes through my jeans like they're not even there, making this hypochondriac wonder if I should get the legs to the hospital to check for frostbite. But the more reasonable part of my brain convinces me that today's spring temperatures are in the fifties. No frost bite possible. And I'm not going back there as a patient, I don't care what happens to me.

I huff to see my breath. It floats like a little cloud rising in front of my face for a second until my escaped air adjusts to the colder air outside and disappears.

I close the eyes so the ears will work better.

There are few sounds I love more than the slapping of rubber against rubber on the running track behind

16

school. With the eyes closed I can almost make myself believe it's the feet I have now hitting the track instead of the two boys running in front of me down the straightaway. I can almost feel the air pushing itself through every strand of hair covering my head. I can almost feel my leg muscles burn with a plea to stop. I can almost feel my lungs filling up my chest, aching when there's no more room for them to expand. Almost.

There's no better feeling in the world.

I've been on the track team since I was in fourth grade, the first year I was old enough to try out. Until this year. This is the year I woke up and found myself in a new body with an added twenty pounds I can't seem to get rid of, and legs that flop around like jelly when I push them to run faster.

I still tried out for the team, but Coach C. pulled me aside after tryouts and told me he was concerned about my health. He said he thought maybe another year to adjust to my new body would help. I know better. I know these new bright white, freckled legs will never let me run an 11:50.02 in the 3,200 meter run like my old ones did.

Now the old Nessa is a ghost. I have her thoughts and memories but that's all that is left. Now everyone makes fun of me because I make them uncomfortable, at least that's the excuse my counselor gives me. I'm like a giant walking joke through the halls of Johnny Appleseed Junior High. The worst thing is that I'm starting to believe I'm the freak the other kids say I am.

Ever since the surgery I feel like I've been split in half. There's me and there's her. I know everything about me, but I know absolutely nothing about her. One of the first questions I asked Doctor Hursh was her name and he said he couldn't tell me. Like an adoption, transplants can be 'closed', meaning her parents didn't want me to know who she was. They didn't want to have contact with me. Didn't ever want to see this body again. I can't blame them, but I wonder if I'd like this body more if I knew a little about the girl it used to belong to.

It happened the spring of my 7th grade year. My grades were good enough; and since I had made it through most of the school year I still moved on to eighth grade after I recovered from the surgeries over the summer. When I came back, no one believed I was Vanessa Meadows. They knew I was in an accident, but that was all. There were news articles about the transplant, but since the transplant was closed they didn't mention the body's name and my mom made sure they didn't mention mine. She played the "she's a minor" card and said she wanted me to

18

live a normal life without the notoriety of being the youngest brain transplant recipient.

Yes. Because what I'm living is a normal life now.

Funny.

I went from somewhat-popular to a freak over summer vacation. I swing my backpack over the shoulder and let the freckled jelly-filled legs carry me into school for another fun-filled, fantastic day.

* * *

Just when I thought there couldn't be anything worse than being "that girl who had her brain transplanted into another body," I've become "that girl who had her brain transplanted into another body and passed out in the cafeteria when she stabbed a needle into her leg."

I pretend not to hear the whispers as I walk through the hallway on the way to my second floor locker, but pretend is all I can do. It takes every ounce of courage I can find to hold the head high and look straight ahead while I walk. What I really want to do is cower in a corner and cry if I hear anyone say anything closely resembling my name.

"Nessa!"

Twin pops her head out from behind my locker door and gives me a toothy smile so bright it threatens to blind me. I smile back, conscious not to expose teeth that aren't quite so perfect. My old teeth were perfect, just like Twin's. The new teeth are not even close.

"How is the Irish Wonder this morning?"

"It fell in the shower and the breakfast burrito I ate before school did not agree with it. Today should be fun."

"As fun as yesterday?" Twin laughs at me, and although 98% of me wants to hit her with a bright white arm, the remaining 2% wins and I laugh instead.

Twin's real name is Maddelyn Rose Sanders, but everyone else at school calls her Maddie. To me, she's always been Twin. Our mothers were friends before we were born and were pregnant at the same time. Before I drew my first breath of air, I had her as a friend. Twin was born two weeks and three days before me. There were other similarities as we got older. We both had dark brown hair, not quite black, but as close as it can get. All through elementary school we kept our hair straight and the same length. From the back no one could tell us apart. There were differences, too. I grew half a foot taller and she had the blue eyes I always wished my brown eyes were.

We're so far away from looking anything alike now that calling her Twin seems stupid. But it's one of those habits I haven't been able to break yet. Maybe I don't want to.

As much as I love her, looking at Twin is painful. She still has everything I lost.

"Maddie?" Cole Mariano comes around the corner and I try unsuccessfully to blend into the wall of tan lockers. He looks into the new green eyes and they lock. Maddie was invited to his party. "Oh, hey… Nessa."

I half raise my hand in a wave but realize he's already looked away so I shove it into my pocket instead.

"Do you have the answer to that question about the War of 1812? I looked. I couldn't find it anywhere in the book," he asks her.

"It's the Battle of Lake Erie, September 10th, 1813," I look at Twin and say. "Wasn't in the book."

Cole and Twin both stare at me.

I tap my head with the index finger. "Same brain, different body."

"Cool, thanks," he says before he takes off back down the hallway.

"Hey, it could be worse," Twin says as she closes my locker. "You could've kept your body and got her brain,

21

and what if she was as dumb as she looks? At least you got to keep the smarts."

I knock into her as we walk and slam her body into the wall of lockers.

"Owwww, Nessa!" she yells.

"I didn't do it, the dumb body did."

3

The Eyes Spy a Car

"Carly, let Vanessa help you with that. And don't forget to ask her in French."

The lungs suck in a big breath. Carly Wilkins has been horrible to me since before I came back to school with this new body. Mrs. Beatty had to know this. She could have told her to ask any of the other 19 students in class, but no. She wants her to ask me.

"I would, Mrs. Beatty, but I'm not sure how to say 'red-headed freckle freak' in French." Carly spins in her front row seat to face the rest of the class. Most of them laugh, making her mouth turn into a clownish grin.

"Carly, that is extremely inappropriate. You can think about how wrong that was during your detention."

Mrs. Beatty's hand shakes as she fills out the detention form. Carly stands up gracefully and saunters to the desk in the front of the room like a supermodel. Her long blond hair sways back and forth across her back as she walks.

When Mrs. Beatty hands it to her, Carly waves it like a flag as she walks out of the room. "Inappropriate, yes. But *so* worth it."

More laughs.

The forehead hits the top of my desk with a thud.

Can this day be over now?

* * *

Twin is waiting when I escape class. I let the body take a deep breath even though I know the air will smell like sweaty gym socks and floor wax.

"Doesn't look like your day has gotten any better," she says.

I shake the head and step into stride with her, walking as far away from Carly Wilkins as possible.

"Do you think they'd let you switch to another class?" Twin suggests after I fill her in on how Carly is going to spend her afternoon.

"When the school year is almost over? I wish. She does know I didn't pick this body, right?" I've been counting how many people look me in the eye as we walk down the hallway to our next class. I'm still at one. And that's Twin.

"You know Carly, she doesn't care about anyone or anything except for herself. Just ignore her," Twin says.

Easy for her to say. Twin still looks like Twin. I look like Ronald McDonald's long lost kid.

"I used to like Carly," I say, a hint of sadness in my voice.

"Yeah, me too. Why do people have to change?" Twin asks before waving and ducking into her language arts class.

I know Twin was talking about Carly. But I stand frozen in the hallway, my books weighing down the arms and her words weighing down the heart.

Why did *I* have to change?

I have all the answers to that question, but none of them make me feel any better. I had to change when I was perfectly happy with everything the way it was. It's just not fair. Not one bit of it.

The bell rings just as I slide the lock into place on the bathroom stall. I'm 98% sure no one will look for me. I can stay here and cry in peace.

* * *

I walk out of the double doors of the school at 2:45 p.m. and vow to look at the bright side like my counselor says I should. No EpiPen was jammed into my thigh today. I gave Cole and Twin the answer they needed for their American History homework. Carly Wilkins is rotting in detention right now. I don't have to go to the emergency room and stare at a freaky TV and ugly leopard-printed heels.

Life is good.

Convincing myself isn't easy. Truth is, life would be so much better if I could sprint home and shove a big spoonful of chunky peanut butter into the mouth. But the semi-truck that hit our car head-on a year ago took those options away from me and I have to accept it. Just be happy I'm alive.

I dig into my backpack, pull out my air pods and shove them into the ears as I wait to cross the street. Music is the only thing that keeps me from thinking too much. I hear people yelling, but the music pumping into the ears muffles a lot.

Usually Twin walks home with me, but she missed a homework assignment and got detention so she's hanging out with Carly and I'm on my own.

Out of the corner of the right eye I see it. There's a white car, going way too fast for being in a school zone.

Suddenly it swerves, heading to the other side of the street.

But then it takes a sharp turn and is on a straight course for me!

4

The Face Is on Camera

Dive!

My brain screams to the muscles, but they do nothing. Not one body part responds.

I'm going to die. Again.

In an instant I'm pulled from behind and fall backward onto the grass. I don't know much, just that the impact wasn't from the car. The back lies against the grass and I don't move. Couldn't if I wanted to.

Someone is lying next to me, and this time when my brain tells the neck to turn that way, it actually does.

Cole.

He's smiling.

"You okay?" he asks.

I don't answer. Every inch of the body shivers, so much that I wonder if the teeth are going to fall out of the gums, and the hands are a sweaty mess, but that's alright. Sweating and shivering means I didn't damage my hypothalamus.

I hit the ground hard. It was one of those impacts where everything hurts inside because it all got moved around when it wasn't supposed to. It scares me enough to make me want to go through the brain checklist Mom helped me come up with. Just to make sure my brain is still okay after the fall. Hypothalamus was number six on the list, so I mentally check that one off.

I stare into Cole's brown eyes to start my cerebrum checks and still see them as brown. The trees behind him are still green. Right brain and colors, check. Twenty-four plus twelve is thirty-six. Left brain and logic, check. My grandmother's name was Amelia Kunkle. Memory, check. I slowly use the arms to prop the top part of the body into a sitting position. No problem staying upright. Just to make sure, I hold my arm straight out at my side and bend the elbow back in so the index finger touches the tip of the nose. Balance, movement, and cerebellum, check. I move the tongue forward and back to get enough saliva in the mouth and then swallow big. Brain stem, check. I'll just have to believe that my pituitary gland is fine. There's no way to check my hormones here in the front yard of the school.

The body breathes a big sigh of relief. The head hit the ground hard and all of the brain stuff attaching it to the body didn't unplug. I'm still alive and able to function.

Life is good.

Cole looks at me like I just climbed out of the ground. With an elephant on my back. I itch the nose a little before I take the finger off of it, trying to play it off.

"Are you okay? Seriously?" He bends the top part of his body up off the ground and props it up with an elbow. "I know you're kind of fragile and stuff."

And stuff? What's stuff?

Instantly there are twenty-five people standing around us and I can only get bits and pieces from what they say.

"…car kept going…"

"…like it didn't see her standing there?"

"…could have killed a bunch…"

"…didn't see the license plate…"

Someone takes the hands and helps me stand. When I look around Cole is already gone, swept up by at least five girls, convinced that he's their hero as well as mine.

And I never said a word to him. Not a 'thank you', not a 'what did you mean by stuff', not an 'I'm not fragile – I'm your worst nightmare'. I really need to work on my conversation skills.

Who almost runs a fourteen-year-old girl down in front of a school with about a million witnesses and doesn't stop and get out to make sure she's alright? Seriously. Who does that?

Someone who wanted her dead, that's who.

When the thought hits my undamaged brain, my hypothalamus kicks into overdrive and blankets the skin in so much sweat, I'm surprised it's not soaking through my clothes yet. I scan through the crowd for anything or anyone suspicious, but there's too many people. The white car is gone. So is any sense of security I may have had before the feet hit that street.

"What's your name?"

The question comes at me quickly, forcefully. So much that it scares me and the body jumps.

There's a woman before me, holding a messy-haired toddler with his legs wrapped around her left hip. She's dressed too fancy for school pick-up. There are pearls around her neck and her blond hair looks like it's a helmet instead of millions of free-flowing strands. A young girl

31

that looks like a younger version of the woman stands beside her, holding up a phone.

I'm really confused. Maybe the brain's not as undamaged as I thought it was. I've practiced this so many times, but I still do the wrong thing. I tell her my name.

"Vanessa Meadows."

The mini blond girl pivots and points the phone at her mother who looks into it like she's reporting for the six o'clock news. "Again, this is June Marks reporting from Johnny Appleseed Junior High School in New Albany where Vanessa Meadows just narrowly escaped being hit by what would have surely been a hit-and-run driver." She looks away from the phone, to me.

"Are you sure you're okay?"

The girl points the phone at me again. Is this a video? I don't want anyone recording me!

The eyes look to the left, then to the right. There's no one to save me from this. I'm beginning to think getting hit by the car may have been better.

"Were you injured, Vanessa?" she asks again.

"No — I don't think so. Just shaken." The voice that comes out of the mouth squeaks.

"You're lucky that boy was there to tackle you. And that, ladies and gentlemen," she says into the phone, "is what we call thanking our lucky stars. Vanessa Meadows must have someone up there keeping an eye on her. I've never seen anything like it in ten years of reporting."

She looks to her daughter and makes a cut-the-throat gesture with her free hand. The girl taps the screen and drops the phone down to her side.

"It's amazing what you see when you pick your kids up from school, huh? Thanks for the interview, Vanessa," the woman says over her shoulder as she carries the toddler back to a large SUV parked a few cars down the street. "Glad you're alright. Be sure to watch yourself on 10TV tonight!" She climbs into the mammoth vehicle and drives off.

The body is frozen in place. It won't let me move a muscle.

I gave them my name. It's going to be on the nightly news. On *television*.

If whoever was driving the white car really did want me dead, they may still get their wish. When my mother finds out that I told my name to a news reporter who's putting my picture on the nightly news, she'll finish the job.

5

The Mouth Eats Some Woman-Crying-at-the-Door Stew

Last night I didn't watch the news to see if I was on it. I kind of wanted to, but couldn't find a safe way to do it. I couldn't take the chance of Mom walking in the room and seeing me on television, telling the world my name.

My nickname for her when she gets like that is 'The Griz'. She's an insanely private, protective person who doesn't want anyone to "know our business". She always says that's why we live in the middle of big city Columbus instead of some small town where everyone knows what type of bacon you fry up in the morning and what time your last light goes out at night.

But this morning I'm pretty sure everyone at school saw me on the news or at least heard about it from a friend. For the first time in a year, people looked me in the eye without cracking a joke. A few of them told me how cool it was that they saw me on or their YouTub channel. Although no one told me how happy they were I was okay.

The last bell rang a few minutes ago, so I'm walking back to my locker when another girl stops me. I can't remember her name. She might be in sixth grade.

"Did you get to see it?" she asks. "I would've been so excited to have a reporter talking to me, I don't think I would've been able to talk."

I want to tell her that 'excited' was the last thing on my mind since someone had just tried to kill me minutes before that, but I keep my mouth shut and nod, hoping if I don't keep the conversation going she'll leave.

It works.

Twin had seen the news. She said I looked good, just a little jittery. Seriously. How does she expect a person to look when they almost get hit by a car? Carly didn't say a word to me in French class. Just sat in the back row, arms crossed over her chest with a look on her face like she was sucking on sour candy. In Carly's case – silence is heaven. And if being on the news last night made me into a somewhat celebrity, Cole became untouchable. The reporter didn't say his name on TV, but you know school. Word travels faster than the speed of light. Everyone knew it was him who pushed me out of the way. I couldn't even look at him from across the cafeteria because there were too many people surrounding him.

My French book is jammed under a pile of paper and other books. Of course it is. That's just my luck since I need it for homework tonight. I lay the rest of my books down on the floor at the feet and start to wiggle it out so the papers on top of it don't fly all over the hallway. I really need to clean this locker.

"Need an escort on the way home tonight?" Cole's face pops out from behind my locker door and scares me so bad that I yank the book out. The papers on top shoot out of my locker like it was a cannon. They cover the floor of the hallway behind us and everyone just walks on them.

I drop the body to the floor and start picking them up, one by one. I glance up to see Cole, kneeling down, helping.

"Thanks, I've got this. I'm getting picked up tonight, so I'm good." I grab a paper that has at least three dirty footprints on it. Hope I don't still need it for anything. I study the dirt designs closely. "And thanks for yesterday." I want to say more, but nothing comes out.

I'm back to standing before he can help me up, and grab the stack of retrieved papers from his hands.

I busy myself with putting them back on the top shelf of my locker, hoping he'll leave.

He doesn't.

I back up to shut the locker door and he's still there.

"You sure you're alright after yesterday?"

I nod.

"Guess you'd better get out there before you miss your ride," he says. The eyes watch him walk back down the hallway and wish I hadn't lied to him. I don't have a ride. I get to walk home today and worry that every car that passes is going to turn its wheel suddenly and try to run me down. And I still didn't thank him for saving my life.

* * *

I don't have to walk home alone. Twin's house is only a few blocks away from mine so I only have to walk alone for the last two.

The eyes watch every car. Every person. Every bird, bug and worm. They look for anything weird or suspicious. With every step the feet take, I figure out an escape. The ditch on the side of the road, a patch of high grass I can hide in if I need to. There are a few trees with low branches I could force this body to climb. Maybe.

But I worry for nothing. I make it home completely safe.

I open the front door to find my mom holding a big, heaping spoon of peanut butter.

The mouth on the face hangs open in disbelief. Is she *insane*? I can't decide what to do – scream in her face or run, crying to my room. Or both.

Instead, I calm down enough to talk somewhat rationally.

"Did you forget where I was yesterday and *why*? I was in the hospital emergency room. Because I thought I ate a peanut. You knew I was coming home; shouldn't you hide the peanut butter instead of eating it right in front of me?" I'm hurt beyond words. She's my *mother*. If she had any kind of motherly instinct at all, wouldn't she pick up on that?

"No, honey." She holds it out to me. "It's for you! I found it at the grocery – peanut butter that's safe for people with peanut allergies."

"No way! That's a thing?" The heart beats twice when it's supposed to only beat once. This has to be a dream.

"It's definitely a thing! Check out the jar! But first, eat this amazing spoonful of peanut butter." Her smile is so bright, I wonder if it'll give me a tan.

I swoop over, take the spoon in less than a second and have it shoved in the mouth before the body takes another breath. I drop onto the couch and give her a fake smile through the stickiness of the butter clogging up the mouth. I fight the gag reflex. Her heart was in the right place, but it doesn't taste the same. It's downright nasty, but I give her a thumbs-up.

"Oh, good. You have different taste buds now, so I wasn't sure if you'd like it as much as you used to."

Maybe that explains it. Guess I'll add that to the ever-growing list of things I lost with my old body – my love of peanut butter.

I take a quick glance around to make sure Mom didn't try to sneak anything in our now-sterile living room. Nothing in here says it's a home, but that's the way I want it. I made Mom put away all of the pictures. On that first day home from the hospital I realized I couldn't handle the constant reminder of my Dad and my old self. Those two things that were taken from me on that one day — I just can't.

All that would be left would be photos of her and what Mom has photos of just herself sitting around the house? So now our house looks like one of those staged houses on the home channel, the ones they're trying to sell so they take away all of the pictures and make the house look sterile.

I drag my backpack up the stairs by its shoulder straps, making it thump loudly with each step it hits.

"There's got to be a quieter way to get that thing up there," she yells from the kitchen. The ears hear her, but it's easier to pretend they don't. I'm just glad she didn't say anything about me being on TV last night. I didn't think about one of her co-workers seeing it and telling her about it. If she knew, I'd be grounded in my room by now.

I fly through my algebra homework in about ten minutes. Maybe Twin is right. It's a good thing I got to keep my brain. I'm putting the finished pages into my folder when the doorbell rings.

"I've got it!" Mom yells from the kitchen. Good, because these jelly legs will take eight years to get me down the stairs to answer it.

But what if it's Cole? What if he was worried about me being 'fragile and stuff' and stopped by to make sure I got home safe? I drop my folder to the floor and make the jelly legs carry me down the hallway to the top of the stairs.

"I'm sorry, but no one with that name lives here," I hear Mom say. Her pleasant voice floats on a cloud of happy to where I stand at the top of the stairs.

"What about red hair? The girl I'm looking for has red hair." The new voice is a woman. Loud and obnoxious. "I saw her on TV last night, she said her name was Vanessa Meadows, but I know that's not true."

"You asked me if Alexis O'Riley lived here and I told you 'no'. I've never heard that name in my life, regardless of what color her hair is or what she said her name was on television." Without seeing the flash of Mom's eyes or the straight line of her lips when she's mad I know the grizzly bear is on its way. Her voice is heating up faster than the microwave.

The body my brain resides in sits down in the upstairs hallway. Normally, I'd be ready for a show - even if it's one the ears hear, but the eyes can't see. Normally, the fact that the Griz is about to make a long-awaited appearance would make me insanely happy. I've missed that crazy mama bear! But nothing about this woman at our door is normal.

She's here to kill me.

It's all I can think of. I'm finding it hard to breathe. I take short, quick breaths instead of regular ones. Should I hide? Should I run to my room and call 911? What if Mom's in danger, too? She's the only parent I have left.

As silently as I can, I run back to my room and grab my phone from my desk. The operator answers right away. I whisper when I tell her we have a trespasser who refuses to leave and need help immediately. I hang up and return to my spot at the top of the stairs. Now I worry they won't get here in time.

"I'm sorry, I think we've gotten off on the wrong foot." The woman sounds calmer now. "I was just wondering if I can speak to the girl with red hair that walked into this house a few minutes ago."

The right hand flies up and the teeth take a bite out of the nail on the middle finger. *What is going on?* I've never bit my nails before. And yuck – these aren't even *my* nails! I should do something, *anything*. But fear keeps the butt firmly attached to the upstairs hallway floor. I don't know if I'm more terrified of the woman downstairs or the fact that I seem to have lost all control of this body.

"You have two wrong feet if you think I'm going to do anything but call the police right now! You'd better turn them around and walk them back down my sidewalk and as far away from my house as you can get."

And — the Griz is back!

There's a pause, long enough to make me wonder what's going on down there, but I'm too afraid to peek around the corner and look.

"I'm sorry, please don't do that. I really need to talk to her about something. She knew my husband. It's very important." Her words are urgent and her voice catches like she's on the verge of tears. It tugs at each tiny string keeping this heart inside this body. Apparently it didn't fool mom.

"Not as important as you leaving my property. Right *now*," Mom growls and my mind pictures her all black and hairy, standing on her hind legs. She's hunched over to fit her large, grizzly seven-foot body inside the front door frame.

The woman is crying now. Her blubbering carries up the stairs and fills the ears.

"You don't understand! I need — (sob) to know — (sob) — what happened. Can you please ask her if she knows anyone from Muncie, Indiana?"

"I will NOT!" the Griz yells and slams the door closed on the distressed woman. I'm surprised it took her that long. I hear the deadbolt slide into place.

"Do you think she'll leave?" Mom asks me. I don't know how she knew I was at the top of the stairs, but she's down there looking up at me.

"I would if I were her. The Griz scares everyone," I say and it's true. Doctors in the hospital would see her coming and run out of my room with their white coats flapping behind them like super-hero capes. And when the Columbus Dispatch got a tip that the first successful brain transplant on a teenager happened in our city, it was the Griz who didn't let them get anywhere near my room. When the article did get published, my name was not mentioned. This Griz is a pretty good person to have on your side when you need her. It also helped that a cure for lupus was released that week which took the headline away from the transplant story, but I still like to think the Griz was the real reason.

The woman's still wailing in the front yard.

"Someone called last night, late. Asked for you by name," Mom says. "I figured it was one of your friends who lost your number. I told them you were asleep and that they'd have to talk to you tomorrow. I bet it was her. How could I have been so stupid? I led her straight to you."

"What was she talking about? Did any of it make any sense to you?" I ask.

"No, what about you?"

I shake the head. "I don't know anyone from Indiana. And I definitely didn't know her husband."

Only a minute or two passes before the sound of sirens grows louder. They stop in front of our house. Multicolored lights flash through the curtains, turning our drab living room wall into one from a dance club.

Mom and I peek out of a small crack in the curtains to see them come into the yard. The woman's sitting by the sidewalk, her legs folded under like a pretzel. When she sees the officers, she lies flat on the ground and makes her body limp when they try to move her. It's the first I've seen her. Her dark brown hair is tangled, but she looks normal in a green sweater and jeans.

One officer grabs her by the wrists, another by the ankles, and they carry her like she's hog-tied to the squad car.

"Are they allowed to do that?" I ask Mom.

"Are you going to tell them that they can't?"

I still haven't stopped shaking and now there's a huge chunk out of one of the fingernails.

"Did you call the police?" Mom asks.

I nod. I never mentioned the car that almost hit me yesterday, she would've taken me back to the hospital. I can't tell her how worried I was that this woman was here to do the now-daily attempt on my life.

Mom looks at me and I'm sure my face is an open book of worry. She can tell something's wrong. But typical for the Griz — she doesn't ask. The Griz is all scare tactics and has little emotion. She makes a stupid joke to cheer me up instead.

"I've got some woman-crying-at-the-door-stew brewing on the stove. Are you hungry Alexis?" she asks.

I laugh half-heartedly at her horrible joke so she doesn't see how completely freaked out I am that this woman who had to be removed by the police from our front yard seemed to recognize me. *I* don't even recognize me.

"Wait, did she say she saw you on TV?"

6

The Hands Try To Deliver a Letter

The pediatric wing at Columbus General Hospital is quiet today. Not silent, but quieter than normal. I don't contribute to the quiet; my sneakers squeak each time I lift one of them to get further down the hall. There are a few beeps from some of the rooms and a few of the nurses talking at the station on the right. They wave and smile when I pass.

I spent a month and a half here; I remember the sounds like it was yesterday. And the smells. Hospitals always smell the same. You don't smell it when you've been in one for more than a few hours and you get used to it, but leave for more than a day and come back. Or go home and smell your hair. Or try to get it out of your nose. Hospital smell.

I turn the corner and almost run into Jaz with her wheelie. It's a pole that your IV bag hangs off of with wheels on the bottom so you can take it with you. Here at General we just call them wheelies. It's much better than saying "my IV bag on a pole".

"Nessa! I heard you — were coming today."

"Jaz!"

Jaz is three years older than me and about a head taller. She looks like she was in a fight -- her eyes are dark around the edges like she got punched one too many times. Her normally beautiful dark skin is gray and ashy. Unhealthy. I try to convince myself it's because of her new wig. It's a bright turquoise blue, brighter than the blue one she wore when I shared a room with her for a week. It's straight and settles right above her thin shoulders. I'm happy to see her, but is it ever good to see someone in the hospital?

We give each other an air kiss so no one gets hurt or passes any germs.

"Fresh delivery?" She looks down at the gift bag in my hand. On the side is an elephant with a colorful polka dotted birthday hat blowing out candles on a birthday cake with his trunk. It holds the eight stuffed monsters I made in time for Monster Monday. Eight's a new record for me.

I'm pretty proud of the fact that someone gave my visit day a name. It means the kids here look forward to it. They look forward to seeing me, or at least the monsters I sew. And I know from experience that there aren't a whole lot of things kids look forward to in this place.

And the best thing? No one here knew the old Nessa. To them I'm just Nessa, the girl who hand-sews cute and colorful monsters for them. Monsters they can hug when shots go in or blood comes out. Monsters who will protect them from the shadows and the weird noises the machines make in the middle of the night. When the only light comes from the crack in a door that doesn't lead to their Mom or Dad.

Word gets around fast, and before Jaz and I get to the common room we've got three kids following us, trying to peek into the elephant bag. I've been doing this long enough to know to stuff tissue paper in the top so each monster will be a surprise.

"Do you have one with horns?" A little boy asks. He's pushing a wheelchair with another boy in it. The one in the chair looks a few years older than the one pushing him. They must be new, they weren't here last Monday when I brought a batch of five.

"I might — I think I had one, but one of the other monsters might have eaten his horns off. They think they're pretty tasty," I tease him. I made three with horns this time. Horns are always a highly requested monster feature.

Both boys giggle.

There are five new kids today.

I start the same way I always do, telling them who I am and how I was here, in room 2458 next to the purple butterfly with the pink spots on the hallway wall. I tell them how after a few weeks I was bored and my mom brought me a needle, thread, some felt and a book of monster patterns. When I was well enough, I started my deliveries. The rooms closest to me got the first ones and as I got better and could walk further I'd deliver to other rooms.

I make my story short. The kids don't care about my history here, they only want the monsters. But I want them to know I was where they are now. And I'm out, and better. Physically, anyway.

The kid pushing the wheelchair gets the first horned monster I pull from the bag. He names him 'Chin Jackson'. I don't ask. Kids come up with some crazy names.

After the five new patients have their monsters, I give the three left to a few of last week's kids that are still here. They like to make families. Monster parents, grandparents, sisters, brothers, and cousins.

I push Jaz's wheelie back to her room with her and help get her blankets situated. We'd only been out there twenty minutes at the most and just looking at her tells me she's wiped.

"So how's the body?" she asks. I can tell she's trying to talk like she's not out of breath when she is.

"Do we have to talk about me? Can't we talk about you? Why are you back?" I ask. What a stupid question. I regret the words as soon as they escape.

"I'm back because it's back — much worse this time. Wreaking havoc — on my lungs. Guess I'm — in the zero percent."

L.E.A.M. is the miracle lupus drug that changed the world. Lupus Eliminator Affecting Millions comes in the form of a pill and repairs the immune system in a matter of days. The headlines and the stories on the news shows brag about a perfect success rate – 100%. Now you can cure lupus faster than a cold.

"Can't you just take L.E.A.M. again? Maybe this time it will get it all?"

Jaz sighs. "I did. It didn't work this time. They said if your body is — immune to the drug there's — nothing — they can do. I'm back — on chemo. I think it's making — me sicker not better."

That can't be true. It just can't be. They said it works on everyone.

"So you're just giving up? BioMed makes L.E.A.M. The company headquarters are here in Columbus! If I were you, I'd be knocking down doors to find out what you can do!"

"Do I look — like I can knock — down doors?"

I feel tears coming but don't want her to see them. Jaz was my favorite roomie. That's saying something – in a month and a half I had a ton of them. She was the one who made up the crystal ball game. We'd each take turns, pretending we had a crystal ball and 'predict' a life for each other. Mine for her were goofy to make her laugh. It always worked. Once I told her she was destined to be a high wire trapeze artist in the circus who fell deeply in love with the lion tamer. Until the lion (who had also fallen in love with her) ate the lion tamer out of jealousy.

Her predictions for me were always sweet. Full of happiness and love. I'd get married, have fifteen kids and live in a mansion. Or I'd travel the world. Live on a cruise ship. Whatever she made up for me would leave me warm and happy. One of the most terrifying places for a kid to be night after night is in a hospital. Having a best friend kind of makes being there bearable.

Jaz had gotten my first monster. It was the crappy one where I was figuring out how to do it and the stitches are all over the place. He's staring at me from the table next to her bed. One of his eyes is higher than the other. She told me he wouldn't be a good monster if his eyes were straight. She named him Sam.

"Love the new hair! I love the color." I try to keep my voice high and upbeat. I hope it isn't overkill. Jaz always knows when I'm trying too hard.

"Yeah, well that's not hard — to accomplish — I dyed that old one myself. This one is — authentically blue. True Blue — according to the — package." She's tired. Her eyes keep closing slowly and she's fighting to keep them open.

"I'm gonna go, Jaz. The Griz is waiting down in the lobby. You know how she gets if she doesn't see me for more than a half hour. I don't need her sending hospital security after me. Stay strong for me, okay? The lion tamer hasn't had a chance to meet you yet." I lean over and give her an air kiss.

"Tell her I said — hi. And do — me a favor."

"Anything," I tell her as I draw a heart with my name on the white board meant for the on-duty nurses' name.

"Take care — of the body. It's — a good one. You're — lucky."

* * *

Mom looks up from her book when she realizes I'm standing in front of her.

"All finished?" she asks.

"Yep." I say cheerfully. Probably too cheerfully.

"Did you forget something?"

"I don't think so."

"The letter?"

The groan that escapes the lips is so loud I wonder if it'll wake Jaz on the third floor.

My mother made me write a letter to Dr. Shayers, or Liz as she told me to call her, thanking her for taking care of me in the emergency room when I got poisoned with the sandwich. I didn't want to write it. I didn't like Liz. And I didn't like her ugly shoes.

But here I am, pulling an envelope out of my back pocket with the name Dr. Shayers written on the front. With a *smiley face* next to it. Because as Mom put it, I should be thankful for *all* of the amazing doctors in my life.

Barf.

The girl behind the front desk doesn't look old enough to be out of school yet. She's chewing a huge wad of gum. It has to be hurting her jaw, chomping up and down so hard.

"Can this be delivered to Dr. Shayers, please?" I ask and hold the envelope out to her.

"Who?" The snapping of her gum is really annoying.

"Dr. Elizabeth Shayers." Mom speaks slow and loud like the girl can't hear at all. How embarrassing.

"I'm sorry, there's no Dr. Shayers here," she answers. She doesn't reach out and take the envelope so I lay it on the counter between us.

Mom laughs from behind me. "You must be mistaken. She saw my daughter in the emergency room here last week."

"Are you saying I don't know how to do my job?" She chomps down on the gum so hard I wonder if it will pull her teeth out.

"I'm saying my daughter was seen by Dr. Shayers last week. She signed off on the paperwork. I just looked at it this morning. How do you think we knew how to spell her name on the envelope? Can you ask someone else?"

"Here. Look for yourself." The girl throws a small book on the counter. It says "Physician Directory" in gold on the front.

The Griz gives her a nasty look and snatches it up. She looks through it for more than a minute, flipping the few pages in it back and forth, scanning it over and over to see if she missed something.

"Let's go, Vanessa." She throws the directory down on the counter and stomps through the lobby to the front doors.

I pick up my envelope and the directory.

"Can I have this?" I ask her. I add some extra sugary sweetness to my words to make up for the rudeness of the Griz.

"I guess? We have a stack of them."

I flip through it just like Mom did in the backseat of our car on the way home. And I find exactly what she found.

There is no Dr. Shayers at Columbus General.

7

I'm Pretty Sure the Feet Hate Me

Mom doesn't know I leave sometimes after she goes to bed. I'm not sneaking out to meet friends or a boy, or to rob a convenience store so I don't think she'd care. Well, maybe she would. She *is* the Griz. And she wouldn't let me walk alone to the hospital to make my Monster Monday deliveries after the crying lady said she watched me walk into our house the other day. That creeped her out.

Tonight the moon makes the little flecks in the school's running track glisten like teeny tiny stars. They're so beautiful I almost feel bad hiding them from the world when the foot lands and covers them up. Even if it's only for a second.

I don't have a stopwatch to prove it, I couldn't read it in the dark even if I did, but I'm pretty sure the new shoes on the feet are helping me run faster. They hurt a little on the sides and a few of the toes. I'm sure the feet are hating me right now. Maybe they won't hurt as much once I break them in. The shoes, not the feet.

Practice makes perfect.

Or at least good enough to get me on the team next year.

I try to think about legs and speed and getting the most traction out of the treads on my shoes, but that word Jaz said earlier keeps filling my brain.

Lucky.

Since the accident I've seen myself as a victim. My body was stolen and they replaced it with a crappy copy. Like someone stealing a Porsche and replacing it with a Kia. But Jaz would gladly take the Kia if it wasn't full of the lupus that's making her so sick.

What Jaz doesn't know is that if I could give this body to her, I would in a heartbeat. Not because I hate it. I'd do it because it would make her better and she's fought way too long.

She deserves this body so much more.

8

The Eyes See a Boy in the Woods

The crying-lady-in-my-yard thing kind of freaked me out.

Okay, not kind of. It *really* freaked me out. And the sandwich thing, and the almost-got-hit-by-a-car thing. I'm collecting these 'things' like an old lady collects cats.

I walked to the school's track in the dark last night, but I held my mace in front of me the whole time with the finger on the trigger. I can't step down a stair without thinking I'm going to fall off of it, and I can't ride in a car without having shortness of breath and white-knuckling it the whole way. Mom offered to leave work early and pick me up from school today but I turned her down. It's much less stressful to walk.

She's alright with me walking home because I always walk home from school with Twin. But I forgot that Twin had to stay at school for a Student Council meeting. She was elected Secretary this year. People vote for you when you look like Twin. People don't vote for you when they don't recognize you. I didn't even try.

Yes, it's occurred to me that someone could snatch me up as I walk home alone. That's why I'm holding my cell phone to the ear, talking to an imaginary person on the other end. It's not even on. I read some news story not that long ago about how someone was worried that the signals from phones could cause brain cancer. Yeah, no thanks.

You'd have to be a complete idiot to kidnap someone talking on a phone. The kidnapped person could yell a description or a license plate number. And when I'm on my phone I don't look like a loser walking home alone with no one to talk to.

"You have *got* to be kidding me!" I fake laugh into the dead phone. I pretend I'm talking to Twin. I keep quiet for a minute, letting the ears listen to the silence of the non-person on the other end. I drop the mouth open like I can't believe what they're saying. Don't judge me. I'm not going to waste my time doing this if I'm not going to be convincing.

The eyes look down in time to see a semi-giant rock in the middle of the sidewalk and I hop over it. It's when they look back up that they see him.

There's a boy standing behind a tree that isn't wide enough to hide him well. His blue plaid shirt sticks out of both sides, along with part of his head. One of his eyes peeks out from behind the tree. He's watching me.

When he sees that I've noticed him he turns around and takes off running into the woods.

I drop my phone into my bag and take off after him.

I know, right?

My mace is in my bag in case he tries something. The jelly legs kick into gear and I'm in the woods before he even realizes I'm behind him. He's a few inches taller than I am in this body, but his legs are faster. Unless he was a turtle, how could they not be? He's so far ahead of me now that I only catch glimpses of his black hair and blue shirt to tell me which way to go. Suddenly, the left ankle twists painfully and the body goes down like a falling Redwood.

It happened so fast I didn't have time to yell 'Timber'.

The head hits a log lying on the floor of the woods and gives me an instant massive headache.

The right hand flies up to the pain right above the ear and comes back down with some bright red, gooey blood. There's not much but it still makes the trees around me spin. I don't know where I am or how far I ran. This was the dumbest idea ever.

I put the legs in front of me and use the log to lean on so I can get back up. But a scream comes out when the twisted ankle sends volts of pain back up the leg. Great. I'm going to die here.

All because a stupid boy looked at me.

I dig into my bag, now lying next to the log, and grab my phone. This time I let the fingers turn it on and press numbers. Get brain cancer from the phone or die in the woods, gnawed apart by a scary animal — I'll take my chances with the phone. As much as I hate this body, it's the only one I've got.

Please let Twin answer. If I have to spend a minute out here in the dark I'll go insane. They'll stick me in a padded room right next to the lady who wouldn't leave our front yard looking for Alana O'Whatever.

"I'm sorry," I whisper when Twin answers. "I know you're in a meeting, but I'm lost in the woods outside of school and I twisted the ankle. It hurts too bad to walk. Can you come help me?"

"That's the weirdest thing I've heard all week," she whispers back. "You still have your find-a-friend enabled?"

"Yep. There's a big rock on the sidewalk, find that then enter the woods there."

"And why are you in the woods?" she asks.

I pause. I know how this is going to sound, but my brain isn't functioning enough to come up with another less embarrassing reason. "I was chasing some guy but I fell and lost him."

"You know there are easier ways to get a boyfriend, right?"

"This is no time for jokes!" I yell into the phone. I'm sure everyone in the Student Council meeting heard me.

"Be there in a sec."

Hopefully she doesn't announce to the room full of people *why* she has to leave. *"I'm sorry, Mrs. Majewski. I have to go. My stupid friend decided to chase a stupid boy into the stupid woods and then she twisted another stupid girl's stupid ankle and can't stand up on her own to find her stupid way back out."*

I try to get up a few times, but the pain is too intense and with this new body I have a low pain tolerance. Sad thing is, I don't know if that's because of the stranger or because of me. Are things more painful in her body? Or is my brain just reacting to pain differently? Sometimes I don't know what is controlled by the brain unless I Google it.

I didn't call the Griz because I'd never hear the end of it if she had to come pull me out of the woods because I used this fragile body to chase a stranger. This way I can just tell her I stepped on that rock on the sidewalk and twisted the ankle. Twin will back me up, even if it's a lie.

There are weird noises out here. I don't like them. Some I recognize like birds and things, but others I don't. The crunching of leaves and snapping of sticks is the worst. Each time I twist the head around to see who's there and no one ever is.

I use some of my wait time doing brain checks. Seems to be okay, which is good because I really knocked my head good this time.

My phone finally rings twenty-one minutes after I hung up with Twin.

"I'm at the rock. You just went straight in?" Twin asks.

"Pretty much. I ran straight in and kept running in a straight line. I think."

"You *think*? I see your location on my phone. Give me a minute or two to find you but I have to hang up with you to use it."

The line goes dead and I try to remember which way I came from, but I'm disoriented. I have no idea.

It's not long before I hear Twin's voice yelling my name.

"Twin! I'm over here!" I pick up a stick and wave it around. Maybe if she sees the movement...

But then hers isn't the only voice I hear. There's a boy talking, too. Did she find the boy I chased in here?

Her bright pink sweatshirt appears from around a cluster of trees. The same second I realize I should have just stayed out here in the woods alone until the animals found me.

It's Cole's voice.

I don't yell again and throw down the stick. Now everything I should do feels dumb. Twin knows I have issues, lots of them. But no one else at school knows the crazy I feel on a daily basis. And I really don't want Cole Mariano in on it.

They find me even though I wish they wouldn't.

"I didn't realize you weren't coming alone," I say to Twin as she sits on the log I tried using to stand up.

"I wasn't sure how hurt you were or if I'd need help getting you out of here."

"And I needed to get out of that room," Cole says.

I had forgotten Cole was our Vice President.

"So — you chased a guy into the woods?" One of Twin's dark eyebrows moves up her forehead like it does when she's confused about something. "Why would you do that?"

"He was looking at me."

"I look at you every day in History and you don't chase me," Cole says flashing me a smug smile.

"I'd never be able to outrun the harem of people that surround you on a daily basis," I say, which makes him laugh.

"I called my mom and told her to pick us up by where you ran in. Can you walk on it at all?" Twin asks.

"If I could don't you think I would've just left the woods instead of having to call you and embarrass myself?"

With one arm around Twin's shoulder and the other around Cole's, they help me out of the woods. The more I walk on the ankle, the better it feels and by the time we reach the sidewalk next to Twin's mom's car I'm able to hobble on my own.

"Hi Nessa," McKenna says as I climb into the backseat. Technically I should probably call her 'Mrs. Sanders', but she and my mom have been such good friends for as long as I can remember, it would be weirder if I called her a formal name.

"Hi, McKenna. Can you please not mention my being in the woods to my mother?"

"Not a problem. But only if you promise me you won't go in there again. It's probably not safe. Especially for you."

I nod as I buckle. McKenna is a graduate of the Griz School of Overprotection.

"You're sure it was a boy and not a ghost or something?" Twin asks once the car drives away. Cole stands on the sidewalk, waving with a smile. I wave back and hope the face isn't the same color as the hair on its head.

I glare at Twin and massage the ankle. The more I rub it, the better it feels. I may not even have to limp when I walk through the front door. The less I limp, the less I'll have to explain to the Griz.

"I didn't see anyone else in those woods," Twin says.

"Of course not, because it took you twenty-one minutes to get there! He's probably in Kentucky by now. And I can't believe you brought Cole." I drop the head into the hands to cover the face.

"It could be worse," Twin says.

"No, it couldn't."

"I could have been on vacation out of state or something. Then who would you have called?"

We both know the answer. And she's right. The Griz would not have been a happy mamma bear.

9

The Fingers Do Some Hacking

This weird calm comes over me when I sew. Tonight I'm being a rebel. I didn't put on the thimble Mom wants me to use so I don't poke the finger with the needle. I've made way over a hundred monsters this year. I think I'm pretty close to being a professional hand-sewer. Professional hand-sewers don't need thimbles.

Or would *she* be the professional hand-sewer? Her fingers are the ones moving the needle in and out of the felt, but it's my brain telling the fingers where to stick it.

Twin sits on the edge of my bed and picks up a few of the felt pieces I've already cut out. I've been trying to teach her how to sew, but she's not very good. She keeps telling me I could do it faster with a machine. Like I don't know that. She doesn't understand that I need to do it by hand. It just wouldn't be the same if I didn't.

"Try to keep your stitches straighter this time, okay?" I say. I think one of her problems is that she doesn't have a lot of patience.

"So what is the brain thinking about as we sew tonight? Strange boys among trees?" she teases.

"Just wishing I knew who this body used to belong to. I still hate it. Would it help if I knew who she was? What she liked and what she didn't?"

"It may make it worse. What if she was this horrible, mean person? Like Carly Wilkins? Then you'd *really* hate the body," Twin says.

"Or maybe I'd be glad she wasn't in it anymore. Like the world would be a slightly better place because of it."

Twin laughs then cries out in pain when the needle pricks her finger. She needs a thimble. She has not reached professional hand-sewer level yet.

"But, seriously." Twin puts her half-put-together monster down on the bed next to her and leans closer to me. The straight line of her lips and the wrinkled skin on her forehead tells me just how serious she is right now. "It bothers me that you still hate the body. It's been a year now. It's a part of you whether you like it or not. It gave you back your life when you almost lost it. Shouldn't you be grateful to have it? I love you, but honestly, I'm getting kind of tired of hearing about it."

If words could slap, there would be a big red welt across the cheek. It takes at least a minute to recover and come up with a response. That's easy for her to say because she's not the one who has to live in this body every day. Maybe I complain too much, but she's the only person I have to complain to! And I thought that if there was one person in this world who somewhat, kind of understood, it was Twin. Isn't that what friends are for? To listen to what you have to say, good or bad?

"I know I should be grateful, but I'm just not there yet," I finally answer. She smiles, but the damage is done.

"I agree then. I think you should find out who she was, if you think it would help," she says.

"But how do I do that? It was a closed transplant. Legally they're not allowed to reveal anything about her to me."

Twin looks down at the threaded needle and felt on the bed beside her.

Thinking about the monster makes me forget what she said at first. But it's one of those things where even when you think you've moved on and forgotten about it, you haven't really. That feeling of hurt still lives in the back of your mind. Tugging from somewhere deep inside, trying to get back out and remind you of it again. And you think you've forgotten about it, but think 'something is bothering me, what was it?' and then you remember. And the remembering hurt is sometimes just as bad as it was when you first heard it.

I may not have forgotten about it, but Twin has. She straightens her back, intertwines her fingers and puts them under her chin. I can't decide if she looks like she's praying or an evil mastermind hatching a plan.

"The sandwich," she says.

I look at her weird and wait for more.

"The car that almost hit you. And don't forget about the lady the cops had to haul out of your front yard who thinks you hang out with her husband in Indiana."

I nod.

"And what about that boy in the woods? Who knows why he was watching you. And you find out that the doctor who treated you in the ER never existed? You don't have to be a genius to realize that your life is in danger, Nessa."

"But why?" I ask. "I sew monsters and wish I could run faster. Why would someone want me dead for that?" Just hearing about those incidents again, all mentioned together seems more threatening. Sweat breaks out on the skin and the right hand flies up to stick a fingernail in the mouth. This time I spit it out and force the hand back down to my side. I close the blind over the window next to my bed. It's still daylight, but I'm paranoid now. I may never open the blind again.

"And that, Nessa, is the question. You didn't do anything that would make someone want to kill you, but what about the girl who owned that body before you? What if she was into something dangerous? What if she had enemies who think you're her because you look just like her? I think that gives you enough of an excuse to take this into your own hands. This is your life at stake here! If you lose this body, they're not going to give you another one."

I nod the head. She's right, they won't. All of the stars were aligned just right when I got this one. Kismet.

"We need a hacker and I know the perfect one."

"Who?" I grab the monster I was working on and curl the body back into the old armchair Mom recovered for my room right before the accident.

"Cole's crazy on a computer. I bet he could at least find her name. We'll never know if we don't ask."

Her phone is out of her pocket in less than a second and she's asking Cole all the right questions. Like she's helped a friend hack into medical records to find the original owner of her body before.

"Here." Twin holds the phone out and the eyes stare at it. She starts shaking it in front of me, mouthing something I can't make out. She can be really annoying when she wants to be.

I grab it and force myself to speak.

"Hi, Cole."

"Hey, Nessa. Do you have a computer there? I'm going to walk you through this. What's your doctor's name?"

"Yeah, I do. His name is Dr. Hursh."

"Okay, get on the internet while I figure out what software his office uses."

So much for sewing monsters. I lay down the one I was working on and walk to my desk for my laptop. I try to ignore Twin grasping her heart and swooning like she's lovesick. It doesn't work so I push her hard off the bed on my way past.

Cole gives me instructions for finding some settings on my computer and once I give them to him my cursor moves when I didn't move it. Like a ghost is in my computer.

I must have gasped.

"That's me moving it," he says.

"You can do that?"

Twin looks over my shoulder as we watch Cole work his hacker magic on my computer. He opens up software that I didn't even know I had and before I know it, there's a prompt on the screen for "Patient Name".

"I'll let you do this part. It's probably your full name. Last name, comma, first name, comma, then middle initial."

"Could this get me in trouble?" I ask.

"I don't know. Maybe? Hopefully not. You're just looking up your own information."

I type in my full name, just like he said.

Meadows,Vanessa

"You forgot your middle initial," Cole says.

"Don't have one." My mom said she couldn't think of a name that sounded good with Vanessa, so they just didn't give me one. It never bothered me before, but now it makes me feel incomplete. Like a part of me is missing. You'd think I'd be used to that feeling by now.

I hit enter and another screen pops up. It's an overview. I die when I see it lists my height and my weight. Not the weight of the old body, but the weight of the new twenty pounds heavier one. Thankfully it's not there long. He clicks on a few more links on the left side of the screen looking for the information we need. Well, *I* need.

"I think I might have found it," Cole says.

It's a form with the words **TRANSPLANT DOCUMENTATION** on the top in bold. There's my name, my address and my mother's signature authorizing the procedure. The form scrolls down and I know I should be surprised when I see her name, but thanks to that crying woman in my front yard, I'm not.

The body belonged to Alexis O'Riley.

10

The Eyes See Puppies

There's a lot of information about Alexis O'Riley on the internet but I can't find any reason someone would want her dead. I find an article on the local news site that says she died from a severe allergy attack after coming in contact with a peanut. Her EpiPen malfunctioned and her brain was without oxygen for too long. It listed her age as fourteen. A year older than I was when I got her body.

Everything else about Alexis O'Riley is puppies. Literally. Her social networking accounts are still active but she had the security set high. The only thing I can see are her avatars which are all pictures of puppies. But that's okay. Perfect, actually. Seeing someone else with an avatar of what I look like right now might send me into the stratosphere.

I follow her on Instagram and Twitter. It seems rude not to since I'm using her body and all.

I scroll down her Twitter page and find a few more recent tweets from people who sound like her friends.

Megan North @megadoo Apr 29
missing @alexisgr8 like crazy 2day. #why

In a brief, courageous moment I send her a private message.

Hi. My name's Vanessa & I'm trying to find some information about Alexis O'Riley. Can U help?

I hope that didn't sound creepy, but the longer I think about it the creepier it sounds.

There's another tweet on her page from a boy named Toby. I send him a PM too and try to make it sound less stalkerish.

Hi. I was friends with Alexis and have a few questions I was hoping you could answer.

I don't expect an answer from either of them but at least I can say that I tried.

11

The Mouth Eats Revenge-Filled Chocolate Pudding

Carly Wilkins, Twin and I used to be best friends before Carly got mean.

I know why she turned into such a mean person, although I don't think it excuses her for doing it. Not last summer, but the summer before that, her mom decided that the mothering-thing wasn't for her and left Carly and her little brother, Mark, with her grandma. As far as I know, they haven't heard from her since.

I get that things that happen to you in your life can make you into a different person. But my life this past year hasn't been pretty flowers and rainbow unicorns, either. I like to think the crappy things that happened to me made me into a better person, not a worse one. I hope so, anyway.

The three of us used to sit together at lunch every day. Without fail.

One day, out of nowhere, she started making fun of one of the younger kids. Laughing about the way he was eating. Twin and I both told her to stop, but she didn't listen. The next day it was someone else for another stupid reason. And every other day for an entire week she had someone else to make fun of or laugh at. She didn't care if they heard her. It was almost like she *wanted* them to.

The next week Twin and I agreed that we'd both enjoy lunch a lot more without Miss Nasty throwing our moods into the trash can. So we didn't sit at our old table. We found a new one and didn't say anything to her about it. She must've got the hint. She never followed.

I figured there would be backlash from her, but I had no idea it would be this bad.

Stupid me, I almost thought she'd feel bad for me after the accident. We both had torn up families in common, right? Wrong. Now she didn't have to make fun of the other kids at school. Making fun of me and the new body was all the fuel she needed.

Now she's standing right behind me in the cafeteria line and I'm frozen in fear.

I usually try to stay as far away from her as I can, but today I forgot to look for her and make sure she was sitting down already before I got in line.

I just need a milk. Since the poison sandwich incident I've brought my own lunch with me every day. There's a tiny lock on it to keep the peanuts out. But today I forgot to pack my drink so my plan is to reach in the very bottom of the milk crate so I can be sure I don't get one that's been tampered with.

I feel the weight of the red frizzy hair lift off of the back. It sends shivers up the spine.

"Do you miss your old hair?" Carly asks behind me. She almost sounds genuinely nice, but I know better. She's saying it louder than a normal tone of voice which means she has an audience. "I mean, your old hair was gorgeous. Even *I* was jealous of it. But this? I have to give you credit, Nessa. If it were me, I would've shaved myself bald. Then I wouldn't be embarrassed to come to school with it like *this* every day."

I feel the hair drop down onto the back but I don't turn around. I look forward, on the verge. Of crying, of screaming, of spinning around and punching her. But I do nothing. I don't like this body or its hair enough to defend it. If Twin had this lunch period, things might be different. She always seems to know the right thing to say to Carly. I do not. There's laughing behind me. Why is there always someone near her who thinks what she says is funny?

I wait for more. Not because I want to hear it, but because I know she's not done. She's still got the added weight to make fun of, or the fact that the skin I have is bright enough to stop traffic. She'll keep at it until I react, making her the winner.

And she almost always wins. I can only take so much before I start to cry.

Instead she screams. It's so loud it hurts the ears and I wonder if they'll ever hear right again. After that, everything sounds muffled. There's laughter behind me and the body turns around to face her even though my brain didn't tell it to.

Carly's hands are outstretched, her face swallowed by horror. Her mouth is hanging wide open. Almost wide enough to catch the dribbles of chocolate pudding making their way down her face from the top of her head.

"I am *so* sorry." Cole says to her, holding an empty pudding bowl in his hand.

"*How could you?*" she screams.

"You were so worried about Nessa having a new hair color, I thought maybe you'd want to try it out and see how it feels for yourself. Mind if I cut?" he doesn't wait for an answer as he slides into the line between us.

This has to be a dream. Did I dream I woke up this morning and came to school instead of actually doing it?

"Mind if I sit with you?" he asks me.

The head shakes a no because I'm positive the mouth wouldn't say it even if I wanted it to.

"I was through the line already, but my pudding jumped out of its bowl and landed on someone's head. And I'm sad because I was really excited about eating it. Do you think they'll give me another one so I don't have to eat it off of Carly's head?" Cole leans in closer to me and cups his hand next to his mouth. He scrunches up his face and whispers 'I have a fear of lice' so loud I'm pretty sure the entire cafeteria hears it.

I can't help it. I laugh harder than I've laughed in a long time.

I know it's mean and normally I wouldn't have laughed, but Carly has been making my life miserable for

85

so long. It's nice to see her get a little payback. I hear a cross between a gasp and a cry behind me and Carly runs off. I hope she's heading to the bathroom. The longer she lets that pudding set, the longer it's going to take her to wash it out.

"If they give me another one, I'll share since you let me cut."

"I still can't believe you did that. Do you have a death wish?" I ask him.

"No, but I wish someone was recording it. 100% viral."

12

The Hands Do What Now?

"Meet me at the food court in an hour," McKenna Sanders says as she ducks into a store.

Twin tried to convince me that I needed a cute new shirt since Cole sat with me at lunch. I know better. Twin just wants a new shirt herself and I was a great excuse to get us to the mall. She said she found this amazing coupon in her locker that she didn't realize she had and it expires today.

We've done this dance eight million times. We'll look around, Twin will find something she 'absolutely cannot live without' and when we meet back up with McKenna in an hour the begging for her new clothes will begin.

Twin's got it down to a science. She almost always leaves with what she wants.

The Griz and I don't work that way. She hates the mall and she hates shopping. When she says 'no', she means 'don't you dare ask me again unless you want to spend the rest of eternity in your bedroom'. Which is why I try not to go to the mall with my mom. But after school today she was in a good mood. Not only did she tell McKenna I could go with them, but she gave me a twenty dollar bill to spend. Maybe she was just happy that we didn't ask her to come with us.

Twin's favorite store, Trendz, is almost completely empty. The mall is usually pretty busy on the weekends, but after school it's silent. The only person in sight is an employee standing behind the register, busy doing something I can't see. She doesn't even look up when we walk in.

"This is my new favorite." Twin squeals with delight. "I just have to have this!" She yanks a cute black and white striped shirt off of the wall.

"Maybe you should try it on first," I suggest. Me, always the voice of reason.

"You're going to find something while I'm in there, right?" she asks. "Your mom gave you cash. You can't *not* spend it." She grabs four more shirts and a pair of jeans on her way to the wall of dressing rooms.

She may know me too well. It's easier for me not to spend money on clothes. When I had my old Nessa body, everything fit. Not only did it fit, but it looked good. Like I was the model they designed it for. But in Alexis's body, nothing fits and nothing looks good on it. There are one too many rolls I feel like I should hide. Now I wear baggy sweatshirts and sweaters. Even in the summer.

I move the hangers on the round rack as I look through each shirt. They're all designed for smaller bodies. Skinny bodies. Old Nessa bodies.

Why did I ever agree to come here? It's depressing.

The sales girl weaves her way through the racks, heading straight for me.

Ugh.

The only thing worse than me trying to convince myself something will look good on this body is a sales person doing it.

"Is there anything I can help you with?" She seems nice enough, her voice doesn't sound fake like so many of the others. Her light brown hair is long and straight. I don't know if I've ever seen someone with hair that long. It covers her entire back. The name tag on her shirt says 'Bree'.

"No, thanks. I'm good."

Bree doesn't leave. She stares at me. "You look familiar. Do I know you from somewhere?"

"No." It's an easier answer than 'Maybe you knew the girl this body used to belong to, but you don't know me'. She starts pushing hangers aside. She holds a few shirts up, sizing them up with my body. I wish she wouldn't. Every time she puts something back on the rack it makes me feel horrible. Like I wasn't good enough for the shirt.

"I bet this would look good on you." She holds up what may be the only shirt in this store that isn't cut to be skin-tight. Bree may have something here. It's a pretty turquoise and has elastic on the bottom hem that should make the stomach area puff out a little and hopefully hide the stomach rolls.

I reach out and take it from her. A flip of the tag tells me it's marked down to $15.99. Perfect.

"Don't you want to try it on? Just to be sure?" Bree asks.

I open the mouth to tell her 'no', but then I change my mind. If I don't like the shirt the Griz will march me back here to return it and get her money back. I think I've mentioned how much I hate going to the mall with my mother.

I turn to the wall with the dressing rooms but Bree steps into my path.

"Those are out of order. You'll have to use the ones in the back."

"Didn't my friend just go into one of them?" I point to the purple dressing room doors behind her. I know I saw Twin heading that way with that striped shirt and about five other things she grabbed on the way by.

"She's in the back, too. I let her know just before she got there. A girl got sick in the middle stall an hour ago and the mall janitor hasn't come to clean it up yet. You are *not* going to want to smell that. Follow me."

She walks quickly, so fast it's hard for me to keep up. The door in the back is behind the counter and she punches in a code on the keypad before she twists the handle. She reaches in to the wall beside the door and flips the light on. I step in and she closes the door behind me.

I look around. This isn't a dressing room. There are shelves and tons of racks, some full of clothes and some empty. This is a storeroom. Before I can consider whether or not I want to get changed in here the lights flip off and I'm thrown into darkness.

An arm wraps around the neck and starts to squeeze.

Is this Twin's idea of fun?

I can't say her name, I can barely breathe. This can't be Twin. She doesn't have this kind of strength. I panic. But only for a second.

The hands reach over the shoulders and grab fist fulls of fabric. My jeans stretch as one knee bends and the body hunches forward. My brain never tells the hands to flip the body behind me over my head and slam it to the floor, but that's what it does. There's a heavy thud and a groan as it hits. I stare at the dark mass at my feet. It doesn't move.

What did I do?

Free of the attacker's grip, I gasp for air and wonder where that came from. I've never taken any kind of self-defense class in my life.

I run out of the room and out of the store faster than I've ever run in my life. And I thought these jelly legs couldn't do it. I don't see Bree or Twin anywhere. I don't see another human being until I'm out in the middle of the mall. I don't know where to go, where to find Twin or her

Mom. Everyone looks at me weird, like they're about to tackle me.

What is going on?

I've held this all in for too long. I collapse on a bench, bury the face in the shaking hands and cry. Hard. I couldn't even tell you for how long.

"Nessa!" I look up to Twin running toward me, with McKenna walking behind. "Where were you? Why'd you leave the store without me?"

"I didn't. Someone attacked me in the back room," I whisper. My arms and legs are still shaking.

"What?" She drops her body onto the bench beside me. "It was so weird, Nessa. I came out of the dressing room and everyone was gone. You and the sales girl. I yelled your name a few times and heard nothing, so I figured you left without me. I was almost out of the store when I ran right into a different girl wearing a 'Trendz' shirt. She said she was sorry, that she had to run out for an emergency, and asked me if I saw anyone else in the store. She was pretty freaked out about the whole thing. You've got to tell mall security!"

"No," I whisper harshly as McKenna catches up to us. At this point I don't know who I can trust and I'm pretty sure the answer is no one. Not even mall security. I try to give Twin a look that tells her not to say anything to her mom. I'm sure I already know what will happen if we go back to the store. No attacker in the storeroom. No associate named Bree.

I should have seen the signs. She thought she recognized me. Wanted me to try the shirt on. Told me the dressing room was out of order even though I was sure Twin went in one. Even the crazy coupon that miraculously showed up in Twin's locker today. How could I have been so stupid?

But the body wasn't.

It knew exactly what to do.

Like it's done this before.

* * *

"Ouch!"

There's no one in my bedroom to hear me yell, but the needle poking through the skin hurts bad enough to make me do it anyway. I should use the thimble. My brain can't concentrate on being a professional hand-sewer tonight.

My phone buzzes with a text and Cole's name appears on the screen.

Twin had him go to Trendz. There has never been an employee named Bree. No one threw up in the dressing room. At that point they thought he was crazy so he didn't even bother to ask if he could look around the back storeroom. He knew they wouldn't let him. Exactly what I thought would happen if I had gone back there.

Three monsters are finished and I've pricked the finger with the needle five times before I remember to check my Twitter account for any messages.

There's one from Alexis's friend Toby.

Hi. Meg wants to talk in person for safety reasons. The main library downtown. 5pm Friday. Meet at the computers. How will we know it's you?

I don't know these people. Not enough to trust that they won't try to kill me. I *really* don't want to meet them in person. I also don't know what Alexis's parents told them. Do they know that her body has a new brain and still walks the streets of Columbus?

It took me forever to convince the kids at school I was really Nessa inside this body. I had to think of past events for everyone, things weird enough for them to realize it was really me in here. I have no history with Alexis's old friends to do that.

But I need to know more about Alexis. More than the puppies and kittens on her internet profiles. Her parents don't want anything to do with me, so Toby and Meg are my only hope of learning more about the girl the body used to be and why someone would want her dead.

Twin convinces me over the phone that it's worth the risk and offers to go with me.

So that's it, I guess. The body gets to see her friends again.

I just wish thinking about meeting them didn't leave me with a feeling in the stomach like twenty of my felt monsters came alive and are trying to claw their way out of it.

I worry for over an hour about what to message him back. How much do I tell him about me? About what I look like? I've seen those romantic movies where two people who haven't met before carry something to help the other person recognize them. A flower, or a favorite book.

Yeah, I'm not going to need that. The frizzy red hair is my flower and the white freckled jelly legs are my book. But I don't tell him that. I don't want to scare them into not coming.

I'll be there. Bringing a friend. You'll know me when you see me.

At least I won't be alone with Twin as my plus one.

* * *

I end up with plus two.

"You've got to let me go with you," Cole begged from across the table at lunch Friday afternoon. "I'm involved now! I'm invested!" And he said his dad could drive us.

Mom was so excited that I was going somewhere with Cole, she didn't pay attention to anything else I said about it. I told her we were working on a report for school, but I'm sure she thinks it's a date. If she knew what we were really doing here, meeting friends of the body's, the Griz might become a permanent fixture in our house. No, thank you. So I keep the mouth shut and let her think she's right.

I've been to the Columbus Metro Library enough to know the computers are on the first floor. Twin, Cole and I don't have to walk far. The place is packed with people. I would've never guessed that Friday night the place to be would be the public library.

"Vanessa?"

I thought for sure I'd be the one to surprise the taller boy walking toward us who looks like he might be around sixteen or seventeen, followed cautiously by a girl our height. But I was wrong. I'm the one who's surprised.

I know Toby.

I chased him into the woods.

13

The Body Was a Badass

"You!" I exclaim, more out of surprise. He's still too far away to hear.

"You know him?" Twin whispers and I nod.

"Hi," I say when they reach us. "I'm Vanessa and these are my friends Cole and Maddie. But you probably already know that since you've been following me."

Cole gives me a confused look that I ignore.

"I'm really sorry about that. I didn't know your name. I didn't know you were the person who messaged me. My friend saw you at a baseball game; he was playing for the other team. When he said he saw Alexis in the stands, like she went to school there, I thought he was crazy. He swore he was right so I had to check it out for myself. But when you saw me behind that tree I could tell you didn't know me, so I ran. I'm sorry."

"It's okay. I shouldn't have scared you off, either."

He holds out his hand for me to shake. "I'm Toby, Alexis's brother."

The five of us just stand there for a minute, not moving, not saying another word. But honestly, in this kind of situation, what *should* you say? *Hi, I'm Vanessa, the girl hanging out in the body of your dead sister. Nice to meet you. Or should I say 'see you again'? Wink.*

"Can we get a meeting room?" I ask.

"No!" The girl behind Toby, who I assume is Meg, whispers and shakes her head violently. There's a messenger bag slung over her shoulder and across her chest. She looks carefully at everyone who passes us like they're about to kidnap us. At least I'm not the only paranoid one here. "Potential bugs," she says and I have no idea what she means. Maybe she's crazier than I am.

"Let's go to the back of the stacks on the second floor. We can keep watch while you ladies talk." He motions to Cole who nods.

The five of us enter the elevator and stand in silence. I'm not sure if they're waiting for me to talk first or if Meg has freaked everyone out too much.

It's kind of obvious by now that Toby's not going to introduce Meg, so I do it for them, hoping to break the uncomfortable silence. "This is Alexis's friend, Meg."

"You even sound like her," Toby whispers.

My heart breaks for him, so much that I'm afraid there's not enough thread in my monster supply box to sew it back up again. I shouldn't have sent him that message. I should've just learned to deal with this body on my own. I was only thinking of myself, not the people in her life who might still be grieving. I can't do this. I want to turn around and leave, but I can't. I'm stuck in an elevator, going up to the second floor.

Twin snickers nervously, making things more awkward when I didn't think it was possible. The door dings and opens in time to save me from saying anything else.

We follow Toby to the back wall of the enormous building. There are four plush chairs arranged in a circle around a small table, hidden by floor to ceiling shelves of books.

"Our mom used to study back here when we were little. She could keep an eye on us and even if we were loud a majority of the people wouldn't hear us. It's the only place I could think of with such short notice." Toby nods at Cole. "We'll keep watch and let you know if we see or hear anyone coming."

Cole nods in agreement and stands like Toby, between the back of one of the chairs and the end of the closest tall shelf. I'm glad he's still close enough to hear us. Just in case Meg turns out to be a psycho or something.

"How are you her?" Toby turns toward us and asks. Meg stares at me, waiting for my answer.

How do I even begin to explain this? His parents didn't tell him that they gave away his sister's body?

"I was in a bad car accident. My body from the chest down was severely crushed. Doctors transplanted my brain in Alexis's body after she was — gone."

Meg coils back into her plush chair. She doesn't say a word, but her mouth hangs open like she started to talk but forgot the words. No one speaks. It's the most uncomfortable minute ever.

"And her parents let them?" she says finally, then looks at Toby. "*Your* parents let them?"

"They signed off on it, yes." I answer to break the silence. "But I'm not supposed to have any contact with them. I'd appreciate it if you don't tell anyone you saw me today. Especially your parents," I say to Toby. "I'm not supposed to even know her name."

"Then why do you?" Toby asks.

"I had Cole hack into the medical records because I think someone is trying to kill me."

Meg's gasp is loud and she exchanges a horrified look with Toby.

"That's why I messaged you," I say. "I need to know why before it's too late."

Meg pulls her bag off and lays it on the table. She digs inside and pulls out a silver flash drive, thinner than a popsicle stick.

"Alexis O'Riley wasn't a normal fourteen-year-old girl," she says. "She created a website called LEAMexposed.com. Have you ever heard of it?"

The three of us shake our heads, no.

"It's an anonymous website with inside information about L.E.A.M. Inside information BioMed doesn't want leaked. About how it doesn't work like they claim it does and how their 100% success rate is completely bogus. Alexis was collecting proof that over time it makes the immune system worse, not better. Worse than the first time they were sick," Meg says.

Don't I know it. Jaz is living proof that L.E.A.M. can fail. And make you sicker.

"Where did she get her information?" Cole asks.

"Our dad works at BioMed," Toby says. "He got her an after-school job cleaning their offices so she could buy some camera equipment and when she was vacuuming she came across some documents she wasn't supposed to see. About how they were burying information about L.E.A.M. that didn't put them in the best light. So she began researching and putting what she found on her website. Anonymously, of course. Since Dad worked at BioMed she was scared that he'd get fired if someone found out it was her. It became an overnight sensation. Her website went viral. But the documents she found weren't enough. She needed undeniable proof. Something that would prove without a doubt that L.E.A.M. isn't the miracle drug they say it is."

Meg stops talking and stares at me again. Up and down, from head to toe. I'm sure she doesn't realize she's being rude. Or maybe she does and doesn't care.

"Once Alexis was killed, there were no more entries. Just like they wanted. When the website stopped being updated, it stopped being promoted and its exposure is nothing now. It's completely buried in searches."

"You think someone at BioMed killed her?" Cole asks.

Meg nods. "Alexis knew it, too. The night before her allergy attack she gave me this drive with her files if something happened to her. I thought she was just being over-dramatic." She pauses, sadness covers her face like a shadow. "She wasn't."

Meg holds the drive out to me but I don't take it. Alexis gave the files to her, not me. Just because I inherited her body doesn't mean I inherited her life or anything she was involved in. Alexis chose to be a rebel. I didn't.

The only reason I wanted to come here tonight was to find out who Alexis was. But now Alexis scares me. She's bigger than I thought she was, and I'm not talking weight here. She sounds too fearless. Too smart. I've never been 'too' anything.

And her friends think it got her killed.

"She wanted me to continue the website if anything happened to her," Meg says, "but I can't. I've never even plugged the drive in. They'll kill me, too, if I do. Alexis was the kind of girl who would take the risk if it would benefit the greater good. But that's not who I am."

"That's not who I am, either!" I tell her. "I don't want that drive. It was a miracle I got this body in the first place, there's no way I'm going to lose it. If you're not going to do anything with the files on that thing, then destroy it."

"I can't. I've tried hundreds of times, but can't do it. If I destroy the files, I'll be destroying Alexis and everything she stood for." Meg begins to cry. "Just having it scares me. I've had it hidden in my attic since she died. Our house was broken into and I'm afraid to leave my house after dark. I think every person that looks at me is trying to kill me for it. I can't live like this."

"I'll take it." Cole grabs the flash drive from her and tucks it into the front pocket of his jeans. "That way you won't have to worry."

She looks up at him gratefully, tears glistening in the corners of her big green eyes.

"We'd better go," Meg tells Toby as she stands. She's been looking at me weird the whole time we've been here, and now she's in a big rush to leave, almost like she doesn't want to be seen with me. Not that I have to be a genius to know why. If my dad walked through the stacks of shelves right now with someone else's brain in his head there'd be a Nessa-shaped hole in the wall.

106

"Nice to meet you — Nessa." She begins to raise her hand, maybe to shake mine, but drops it back to her side quickly. Yeah, it would be creepy to touch her dead friend. I get it. "I'm sorry, it's just so weird seeing you — I mean her — you? I don't know."

I nod. I didn't expect us to be friends after this, so it doesn't upset me much. She looks at me pretty much the same way the other kids at school look at me. Like I'm a freak. It's been a year and I'm used to it.

Toby walks over to me and wraps me in an awkward hug. He doesn't say a word; he doesn't have to.

Their backs are to us, halfway down the aisle of books when I call after them.

"Did Alexis know karate?"

Meg keeps walking but Toby stops and turns to face me.

"She was taking self-defense classes. So she could defend herself if something happened."

That's what I thought.

Kind of comforting to know they worked.

* * *

The nurse outside of Jaz's room motions me over to the nurse's station. I assume to tell me Jaz is asleep. It's too late for her to be getting her treatments.

Instead she hands me a fat envelope with my name written on the front.

"What's this?" I ask.

"Open it."

It's cash. A whole stack of bills. I fan the thumb through fives, tens, twenties, and two fifties.

I have no words. I'm more confused than if the envelope were full of applesauce, dripping all over the hands.

"From parents. Quite a few donated money for you to buy more supplies to make more monsters."

"Supplies? This is enough for my college education!" I say.

She laughs. "Well, not quite, but they wanted to help you out. Your monsters are a hit."

I try to hand it back to her. "I'm sorry, I can't take this. I don't do it to get paid."

"I can't return it. Most of the people that donated don't have kids here anymore. If you don't take it, I'm going to have to put it in the hospital's general fund and they'll replace the carpet in the lobby or a window or something boring like that. Maybe you can find something better to do with it."

I sigh big and put it in my bag, defeated. But I won't pretend there isn't a big smile on the face as the body walks away.

"You know it's Friday night — not Monster Monday, right?" Jaz asks me when I stick the head into her room. She's got her headphones on and pulls them off when she sees me. Her mom looks up from a crossword puzzle book and waves from her chair by the window.

"Hey, Mrs. Lewis. I came because I have news about the lion tamer."

"He loves me, he already told me. You're too late." Jaz's smile is back, it looks weak, but it's there. "I wish you would've called — and told me you were coming, I would've put on the wig — before you got here."

"You know your bald head doesn't bother me. I'm a fan of the natural look. That's why I haven't gone platinum blond with this mess." Her head still has a few patches with hair, but it's thinned out so much it looks more like patches of dirt than hair. It doesn't bother me, just makes me sad. "Seriously, though, I have something I need to talk to you about. Pretty important," I say as I drop the body into the chair beside her bed and give her the bag of jelly beans I brought. They're her favorite.

"Yeah?"

"Jaz, since Nessa's here I'm going to run down to the cafeteria and grab a snack, okay?" Jaz's mom stands up and waves as she leaves.

I wait a few minutes to make sure she's really gone, then tell Jaz everything that's happened to me starting with the sandwich, and ending with the meeting I just came from at the library. As soon as I got home I convinced Mom to bring me here. I told her Jaz called and needed an emergency bag of jelly beans.

"This is too — dangerous for you. Cole has to — get rid of those files," Jaz says.

"That's what I told him. He says he's going to burn the drive tonight."

"Good."

"I just needed to talk to you and make sure you thought it was the right thing to do."

"It is. I also think — he should make a video of you — destroying it and post it to her — website so BioMed knows — you got rid of them. Maybe then they'll — leave you alone. What did your doctor — say to you that day? Oh yeah, kismet. You getting that body — was kismet. It's not

110

going to happen — again so you've got to do everything — in your power to keep it — safe."

My visit lasts another ten minutes until she starts coughing and can't stop. A nurse comes in to help and I sneak out as soon as her mom comes back in. My mom's probably downstairs grilling the receptionist on why there is no Dr. Shayers in the physician's directory. Knowing the Griz, she's probably on the phone with the president of the hospital by now.

I press the down button and wait for the elevator to climb three stories to pick me up. It gives me time to think about what Jaz said.

It was kismet that I got this body.

Kismet.

But did I really get it? Is it truly mine now?

I've been thinking of it all one-sided because one side is all I've ever known.

Now there's another side to this story. Alexis's side. And hers seems so much bigger. So much more important.

I always thought it was kismet that Alexis's body was here for *me*. But what if it was the other way around? What if it was kismet that my brain was here for *her*? What if the fate of the body and the brain becoming one was for something bigger? A greater plan? Alexis's plan.

111

"Cole," the lips speak into my phone as soon as he answers. The elevator dings and the door slides open in front of me. "Don't burn that drive. I'm going to need those files."

14

The Mouth Tells a Big Lie

The park by Twin's house is usually packed on Saturdays so we go early to avoid the crowds. It's the only safe place we can think of to go through the files on Alexis's flash drive.

Cole says the encryption on it is complex and he's trying to break it on his laptop at one of the picnic tables. While we wait, Twin and I swing on the massive swing set. There's no one here so we don't have to fight any kids for our turn like we did when we were eight.

I pump the jelly legs like I remember doing with my own legs years ago when we'd have swinging contests to see who could go highest. Maybe that's how my legs got so strong for track. Maybe I should come here more often. Maybe these jelly legs just need some swing conditioning.

The hair flies up to the sky when I make a downswing. The wind pushing it away reminds me of how I feel when I'm running. At peace. Like the only care I have in the world is this wind pushing through the strands of hair that used to belong to Alexis.

I've hated every red strand of this hair for almost a year. Did Alexis like her hair or did she hate it as much as I do?

The more I get to know her, the more I think she worried more about the world and its people than what she looked like. That was never me. Now I don't know who I am.

"Got it!" Cole yells from the pavilion and I get one big pump of the legs in and use the momentum of the upswing to let go and propel myself into the air. The feet meet the dirt with the skill of an Olympic gymnast dismounting the balance beam.

"Girl, you got some air," Twin yells from her swing.

I'm already to Cole, looking over his shoulder at files flashing open on his laptop screen.

"You're absolutely positive you want to do this?" he asks me. "Once you see this stuff, you can't un-see it."

"100%," I've never been so sure of anything in my life.

"They're really going to come after you once you start this up again."

He can warn me all he wants. I've lost track of how many times they've tried to kill me; it can't get much worse than it already is. I'm not changing my mind.

Cole stops opening files from the drive and turns to face me where I stand behind him. "You know that who you are has nothing to do with the body you're in, right?"

His words were sweet, but wrong.

"Actually, I'm beginning to think who I am has *everything* to do with the body I'm in."

I don't think he understands, but that's okay. He's not living in someone else's body so I don't expect him to.

"Can't believe you two missed my spectacular dismount," Twin says when she joins us. "So, what's this top-secret information that had to be encrypted?"

"Looks like a lot of medical files for people I don't know," Cole says. "I'm assuming they're BioMed patients who've taken L.E.A.M. Here's a screen shot of a news article. Some researcher named Dr. Seymour Rice died in a car accident almost a year ago. And here's another article." He double-clicks the file and a bunch of words fill his screen. "It's about Fiona Gray who works for BioMed. She's the head researcher who discovered and developed L.E.A.M. Here's the problem. Everything Alexis has here is more than a year old. I don't know how relevant it's going to be or if anyone is even going to care about it now. You could spend years tracking these people down to find out if they're still having issues with L.E.A.M. or if their lupus came back."

"I don't have years. I don't even have weeks," I whisper.

I don't know how much time Jaz has left.

"If I went to BioMed..." I say.

Twin interrupts me sharply. "I'm not so sure you should be getting mixed up in this whole thing. If it were me, I'd have burnt that drive by now. A girl already died because of it. Why would you want to take the chance of the same thing happening to you? Don't you have enough drama in your life as it is?"

Again with the slapping of the words. And in front of Cole this time?

"When you have one of your best friends really sick after she was promised a cure, then come back and tell me what you'd really do," I say with bite. If Jaz needs me to knock down BioMed doors to find her another cure, I will.

Because now I have a name of the person on the other side of the door. One who can hopefully fix this mess.

Twin gives me a nasty look then returns to her swing without another word.

* * *

"Are you ready to get some answers?" I ask Jaz when I push the empty wheelchair into her room. Getting her released for an hour was harder than I thought it would be. I told the nurses I was just going to stroll her around the parking lot. Technically it wasn't a lie, I *am* going to push her through the parking lot. I'm just not going to stop when I get to the end.

"I'm just excited — to get out of here and — breathe fresh air," Jaz says. Her blue wig is on, and it's the first time I've seen her wear normal clothes instead of a hospital robe. "I haven't done — a stinkin' thing today so — I could save — my strength."

"Well, you look great," I tell her as I help her from the bed to the wheelchair. I don't have to lie, she looks a little better than the last time I saw her.

"I do?" She rips the wig off of her head and tosses it onto the bed. "I don't want — to look great. I want to look

— like I'm almost dead — so they know what — they're doing to people."

When researching them last night I found out that BioMed's headquarters was just down the street from the hospital so we're there within fifteen minutes. Which is good. If we're gone for too long someone will send security to find us in the hospital parking lot.

The arms push Jaz's wheelchair through the double glass doors. We get plenty of stares in the lobby on the way to the information desk. I'm sure they're not used to sick people in wheelchairs actually showing up in their lobby.

I try to keep my concentration on not wrecking the wheelchair, but it's hard. This lobby is insane. Everything's bright white, not a speck of dirt anywhere. And the ceiling is at least ten floors high with two glass elevators side by side. There are people inside, some looking down at us as they rise to a higher floor, some busy looking at paperwork or talking to each other. Almost everyone in this building wears a white lab coat. We're really out of place here.

"Welcome to BioMed. How can I help you?" A man in a suit behind the information desk asks politely. He has a shiny nametag that says BRUCE. His glasses keep sliding to the end of his nose until he has to push them back up again. I wonder how many times he pushes them up in a day.

"We'd like to see Fiona Gray, please." I try to make the voice even so the nerves don't take the words and wobble them up. I get the feeling that the right hand wants to stick a fingernail into the mouth to calm me down, but there's no way I'm doing that in the middle of the BioMed lobby. I stick the hand into the front pocket of my jeans so I don't have to worry about it. I have more important things to worry about. Like what I'm going to say to this woman once we're standing in front of her.

"And who, may I say, is here to see her?" His smile is genuine. Sometimes you can just tell.

"Jasmine Lewis." Jaz sounds so strong, so sure of herself.

"Thanks, let me see if she's available." He runs his finger down a printed list and punches some numbers on the phone, then speaks quietly into his headset. His words are too quiet to hear. Well, that's a good sign. That must mean she still works here. "I'm sorry," he finally says. "Ms. Gray is in a meeting and can't be interrupted right now. She'll be back in the office tomorrow if you'd like to try again."

We may not have a tomorrow!

If they find out we left the hospital grounds they'll never let me wheel Jaz out of her room, much less the hospital or the parking lot.

The thought pops into my head like a firecracker and spills out of the mouth before my brain has a chance to dissect it first.

"It's important. Mr. O'Riley sent us. He asked us to speak with her immediately."

His body stiffens like someone stuffed a board up the back of his shirt to keep him straight.

"Did you say Mr. O'Riley?"

I nod.

"I'll let her know." He punches numbers into the keypad again and argues quietly into the headset. "Ms. Gray will be right down to see you," he finally says. "You can wait over there." He points to a few empty couches and chairs arranged in a square waiting area.

It was a complete and giant lie, but it paid off. Toby never said what Alexis's dad did for BioMed, just that he worked for them. He could be the janitor for all I know. Whatever he does, he must have some pull if it gets Fiona Gray on one of those glass elevators.

The elevator closest to us stops at the fifth floor, empties, then fills back up again. Is she on it? Everyone looks the same with their white coats on, how does anyone tell anyone else apart?

My brain freezes. The right hand flies out of my pocket like a rocket and I've bitten a chunk out of the nail before I can make sense out of what the eyes see on that elevator heading down to the lobby.

Leopard-printed shoes that could kill someone in a back alley. Leopard-printed shoes I've seen before on the feet of the fake Dr. Shayers.

15

The Body Takes an Elevator Ride

I can't tear the eyes away from the shoes. They step out of the back door of the elevator, then come around the corner and pause when Fiona Gray realizes it's me who is in the lobby asking for her.

Finally the eyes release their hold and take in the rest of her. She's wearing a white lab coat, just like she wore when I saw her in the hospital, but the long hair she kept flipping is gone. Her dark hair is cut into a neatly styled bob that almost looks like a helmet.

She walks slowly to where we sit on and next to the sterile couches, waiting for her.

"Hello. You," she looks down at Jaz, "must be Jasmine."

Apparently Jaz isn't in the mood for formalities. "I need a cure. I took L.E.A.M. — and it made me — worse, not better."

Fiona ignores Jaz and looks directly at me, with her narrow, green cat eyes.

"I'm afraid I didn't catch your name?" She holds a hand out to me for a shake.

I don't take it.

"You know my name," I say with the deepest version of the voice that will come out of the throat.

One side of her mouth lifts into a sneer. I get the feeling she doesn't like me. The feeling's mutual.

"Miss *Meadows* isn't it?" She glares at me, then flashes a smile so fake it could get her arrested for counterfeiting.

"We need answers," I say. "Jaz is really sick. She needs another cure for her lupus."

Fiona looks around us and says quietly, "There is no other cure."

"Then how can you market a product as having a 100% success rate when Jaz is living proof that it can not only fail, but make it worse?" The voice coming out of my mouth is rising, making many heads in the lobby turn to look. Fiona may not want anyone to hear about this, but I do.

"It's not my drug that's not working. There must be something else wrong with you, preventing it from working as it should," she says to Jaz. "What's wrong with your bodies ability to let the cure work is not my fault. There's nothing I can do for you." She pivots quickly in her heels and they hit the floor, clicking with each step she takes back to the elevator.

"Just so you know," Jaz yells as loud as she can from her chair, tears streaming down her flushed cheeks. "My blood is on your hands!"

Fiona yells over her shoulder. "Bruce, call security and have them escorted from the premises."

Bruce punches a few numbers on the keypad and I take off running toward the elevator. I only slow down to take the corner without throwing the body into a wall and find that she's the only one behind the elevator, waiting for the door to open. I skid to a stop right in front of her.

124

Fiona looks at me, surprised for the first second, smoking hot angry for the next. "I can't believe you used your dad's name to get me down here."

"He's not my dad," I say.

"Whatever. He faked your death to save you. You're a liar." she says. The elevator dings and the door opens.

"You're marketing a cure that doesn't work. Wouldn't that make *you* the liar?" I ask.

She grabs the front of my shirt and pulls me into the empty elevator with her. I try to tug loose, but she's got a better grip on me than I thought. Once the door closes completely she lets go and I'm free. But only a little free. I'm still stuck in this elevator with her.

Fiona hits the 12 key and I know it's going to be a long ride.

She looks through the glass enclosing us and throws a Miss America wave and a giant smile to Bruce down at the front desk. While she's busy waving, she's talking, knowing only I can hear her. "Your dad. Most days he likes his coffee black. But every once in a while he asks his secretary for a little cream. I really hope that someday nothing happens to it. You know, like if it were to get spoiled... or poisoned..." Fiona points to someone going

125

down in the glass elevator next to ours, then gives them a thumbs up with another giant, blinding smile.

"So here's what I propose to you, Alexis. We trade. Rice's research for your dad's safety and for yours. I will guarantee it. Consider me a personal, 24/7 body guard. You can go back to being you! Re-enter the land of the living and quit pretending to be... what was it again? Vanessa?"

"I have no idea what you're talking about," I say.

The elevator dings our arrival at the 12th floor.

Fiona leans over and whispers into the left ear as the door slides open. "Research for safety, Alexis." She pulls back and steps out of the door. I hit the lobby button quickly but she's looking in on me as the door slides closed between us. Smiling at me. Then her mouth opens to give a few parting words as her cat-eye winks.

"And don't forget... I know how much you *love* peanuts."

* * *

I'm exhausted by the time I get Jaz back to her hospital room. People dragging you into elevators and threatening you can do that to a person. I'd call Mom to come get me, but I still have six monsters to give out.

There's more noise in the halls this week. Six monsters may not be enough. I might have to give out I.O.U.'s.

I cut my story short – the kids never want to hear it anyway – and pass out the monsters as fast as I can without throwing them. There are six new kids. I made just enough. I'm sure I won't be getting any 'tips' today, but I'm fine with that. I just want to check on Jaz one more time and go home.

With my stellar luck lately, there's a girl in a wheelchair who wants the long version of my 'I was a patient here' story. She introduces me to her older brother, Luis, who pushes her chair. He never says a word. Not even a 'hi'. I try to answer her questions with short answers so she knows I'm in a hurry, but I don't think kids catch onto that stuff. It takes another ten minutes for me to get away.

Finally, I run to Jaz's room. I misjudge my running stop and slide into the door with a crash.

"You okay after tonight?" I ask. "I thought for sure she'd be able to help..."

"It was a chance," Jaz says. "And chances — don't always work out — the way we want them to."

"I'm going to update Alexis's website," I say. Up until an hour ago, I wasn't sure I still wanted to go through with it. A successful trip to BioMed would've meant that I didn't have to start the website up again. But the things Fiona said to Jaz made me realize that it has to be done. She won't admit that L.E.A.M.'s a danger, so someone else will have to do it. And that someone else is going to be me.

"I knew you would."

"You did? You told me not to!" How does Jaz know more about me than I know about myself?

"Yeah, but you always — think with your heart."

"Not always. I had to think about it. Maybe because the heart I have isn't really mine." I place the hand on the chest over where the heart would be. It beats through my thin shirt.

Jaz laughs a half laugh, half cough. The hand reaches for the cup of water on the table beside her bed and gives it to her, waiting for her to stop. I remember the last time her lupus flared up like it was yesterday. She had the bed closest to the window when they moved me in and I was jealous. But the first thing out of her mouth was an offer to trade beds. I turned her down, of course. She says I think with my heart, but she's wrong. That's who *she* is.

That was before she took L.E.A.M.

Her lupus was bad back then, but nothing like this. She didn't cough like she was going to spit out one of her lungs.

"So, enlighten me — you're going to start — blogging as Alexis..."

"Here's the problem. I don't know what to write about. The files she gave us have medical files of people from over a year ago. I have to start tracking these people down to see if they're still having issues with what L.E.A.M. did to them. It's overwhelming. I don't know where to start. Oh, yeah. And I don't have a car or a driver's license and the Griz tracks my every move. If she knew what I was up to — well, you know how not-pretty that would be."

Jaz nods and laughs a little at the Griz comment but then she gets quiet. Not like passing out quiet, just thinking quiet.

"You'll have to — use me."

"What?" I ask. The ears must not be working right.

"Use me. I'll be your — first website feature. You can get my — medical files and post them — out there for everyone to see. You can even have — my chart — at the end of my — bed. I don't know what's on it, but maybe it will help."

I jump out of my chair, shaking the head. "The lupus is doing something to your brain, Jaz. They're trying to kill me, can you imagine what they'd do to you if I plastered your medical files all over that website?"

"Put my picture — and my name. The more you — tell about me — the better. No one will lay a finger on me — because the world would know BioMed was— guilty if they did. No one knew — Alexis when they — killed her, but the world — will know all about me."

"There's no way." She forgets that I know what these people are capable of. Alexis died. And I'm pretty sure Fiona Gray just threatened to kill Alexis' dad while we were in the elevator. "I won't do it."

"Nessa, last Monday — you wanted me to fight this. Knock down BioMed's doors. Well we knocked today — and got nowhere. So we'll try it — a different way. This — is me fighting. You have to do it. Every day you wait — more people take — the meds. Do it tonight."

"What? I can't put it all together that fast." She's crazy. It's like six-o'clock already. Mom and I haven't eaten dinner yet.

"Have Cole help you. He will. Tell him he — has my permission to hack in — and get whatever — files he needs." Jaz reaches to the table beside her bed and grabs her cell. She doesn't smile when she looks into it and snaps a selfie.

"Do you want your wig?" I ask her.

"Are you kidding? That thing — makes me look good. I want everyone — to know how I really feel. Have Cole — send a press — release everywhere. Tell them — they can call for interviews — tomorrow." She uses that smile she was saving from the selfie.

And I show her mine.

16

The Ears Hear My Name

I push the legs harder than I ever have before but the stopwatch shows no improvement. I don't get it. The track isn't wet, it hasn't rained in days. And I've never felt more sure that I can do this than I do right now. But it hasn't helped. The jelly legs are still slow.

I collapse into a heap on the synthetic rubber and suck in all the breath I can. The lungs actually hurt from putting them through so much. At least I've broken in the shoes, the feet don't hurt half as much as they did last time I tried this.

The track isn't lit at night but the lights from the teacher parking lot stretch enough for me to see where I'm running. It's still dark enough to see the stars when there aren't clouds hiding them.

I lay the body flat on the track and look up at the sky. It takes me a minute, but I find Sagittarius and smile at my dad. I wonder what he'd say to me if he knew what I was doing with Alexis's website. Would he tell me I was crazy or would he think I was brave? Right now I feel like I'm a little of both.

I published Jaz's information to Alexis's website about an hour ago. Within minutes Cole had a press release sent out to all of the major news outlets, local and national. Alexis had a press release template on the drive so he just had to fill in the details. The internet traffic to the site was immediate, so high that it took down the entire site. Cole got it back up within minutes. Alexis had instructions on the drive for that, too.

I still wasn't convinced that exposing Jaz was a good idea, but Cole agreed that it was the only way. He said it could take days or even weeks to find someone from Alexis's list of names and then we'd still have to get their permission to publish the data. Jaz is here now, ready to fight.

I didn't ask Twin. I feel like I already knew her answer and it wasn't one I wanted to hear.

"Vanessa?"

I hear the man's voice, but I don't see him.

Slowly I rise from where I lay on the track and turn toward it. It came from the bleachers which are shadowy and dark. The perfect place for someone to hide who doesn't want to be seen.

I left my purse on them with my mace inside and can't get to my purse without him being able to jump out from the shadows and snatch me up. I can't even call anyone for help, my phone's in there, too. The Griz is going to kill me if this guy doesn't first.

I freeze on the track. Paralyzed. I don't know what to do.

His feet enter the light first. Fancy, shiny black shoes. Then tailored pant legs. The rest of his body steps into the light and my mouth opens and speaks a word my brain didn't process first.

"Dad."

Not my dad.

Alexis's.

17

My Brain Learns About Its Predecessor

"You still look like her," Mr. O'Riley says. The moonlight reflects itself off of the tears threatening to form in the corners of his eyes. We're sitting, facing each other, legs folded in front of us in the middle of the track. He looks funny sitting that way in a suit, but I'm not going to tell him that. I've only just met the man. Kind of.

I don't know how I knew who he was. I've never seen him before in my life, but something about him was familiar. I wish I could explain it better, but I can't.

I just *knew*.

His hair is dark. It makes the graying hair around his face stand out. A face that looks a lot like Alexis's. They both have big eyes and a thin nose.

"Can you tell me about her?"

Mr. O'Riley closes his eyes and points his face to the sky. Like he's looking up to her. Like I just looked up to my dad.

"Most little girls love dolls. Not Lexi. She didn't want anything to do with them. But give her a stuffed animal — she had hundreds of them. And she could tell you exactly what store she bought it from or who gave it to her as a gift. And names. She knew each one by name."

He pauses and stares past me into the darkness.

"Lexi was smart, but her grades were horrible. She was a dreamer. Always thinking about something else instead of what she was supposed to be concentrating on. There wasn't a week that went by without us getting a call from one of her teachers. Truth is, Lexi ran circles around us. We tried to keep tabs on her but it was impossible. After a while we just stopped trying. I had no idea she was behind that website until after she — died."

He stops to pull out a tissue from his pants pocket, then continues. "She was also the sweetest person you'd ever meet. She loved taking pictures. She'd take silly ones of herself and leave them for me on my desk or on my phone. When someone like that leaves you it's hard not to feel like you have a giant hole right here." He puts his hand over where his heart would be.

I place my hand over her heart just like he did.

I know. I have the same hole. It formed the same day I woke up and my world was Dad-less.

"I'm sorry." He laughs. "I'm probably boring you. All parents think they have the best kids."

This may be the weirdest experience I've had in this body. My brain is completely uncomfortable talking to this man it's never met, yet the body takes the nerves and soothes them so I'm comfortable. Like I've seen this man every day of my fourteen years. One second I feel like I can't talk to him and if I do I'll say something stupid, but the next I feel like I can tell him anything. Like I *have* told him everything before, so why stop now?

Shy Nessa being overpowered by Alexis who just wants to talk to her dad.

He feels like home. Just not one I'm familiar with.

"Not at all," I tell him. "It's nice to know more about her. When I woke up in her body I hated it. Hated every part that you probably loved. I've wondered if I would've known her, or at least known about her, if I would've had an easier time dealing with the whole thing. The more I hear about Alexis, the more I like her. Which kind of makes hating this body impossible."

"I'm sorry about that closed transplant thing. It seemed like a good idea at the time. And Lexi's mom was having a really hard time dealing with everything. We never thought about how it would impact you."

Would things have been different if I would've known about her from the beginning? I'll never know.

"How did you find me?" If he could find me on the track tonight that means I'm not safe coming here.

"I followed you. The doctors had given us your address in case we ever wanted to get in touch with you. Your mother has our address, too. Just in case. A few people recognized you at BioMed today. Can you imagine what I thought when they told me they saw Alexis in the lobby? When I saw on the news that there was a new feature on the website I figured it was you who put it up. I knew I had to talk you out of this."

"Because you work for BioMed?" I ask.

"Because someone killed my daughter for doing the same thing. I should've been able to save her but I didn't know any of this was going on until it was too late. I've hired so many private detectives, trying to get more information, find out who killed her. I have my suspicions. But it all comes down to the fact that there's not enough proof. This person is smart, very good at covering their tracks. If I would've known what Alexis was doing I could've helped her. Maybe I could've saved her. I can't let it happen to her again — I mean to you."

"I'm not doing this for the same reasons Alexis did. The girl on the blog tonight, Jaz, is one of my best friends. She's really sick and I can't sit back and watch her struggle. I know what I'm doing and I know what the risks are. But I appreciate you being here, trying to talk me out of it."

"Exposing L.E.A.M. won't save her, you have to know that. If she's had a bad reaction to it there's not much anyone can do."

"But I couldn't live with myself if I did nothing. I don't want what happened to Jaz to happen to anyone else. What can you tell me about Fiona Gray?"

He looks at me for a long time before he answers. Like he's figuring out just the right words to say. Or is he trying to make evil look less evil to a fourteen-year-old girl?

"BioMed is a good company. A great company. And Fiona Gray is a great researcher. She developed L.E.A.M. with a lot of late nights in the lab. But she didn't do it from goodness in her heart. In fact, I've known her for a long time and I'm not sure there *is* any goodness in her heart. She developed L.E.A.M. for the glory. She knew it would make her rich and famous. She loves the attention, the awards, the appearances where they make her out to be a genius and a saint, and especially the money she's made from it. She's a billionaire thanks to L.E.A.M. We've had complaints about the drug. I'm the Vice President and I've followed up on a few. But the complaints disappear. The patient improves or we can't find them to follow up."

He pauses.

"When I said I had my suspicions about Alexis' death, Fiona Gray is at the top of my list."

I breathe a sigh of relief. I've been wanting to tell him about our visit to BioMed today, but when he mentioned that he's known Fiona a long time it crossed my mind that they might be friends. And that he might not believe me if I told him what happened. But I don't think that now and tell him about my elevator adventure.

He groans. "We have cameras in the lobby, but none that show the elevators. Of course, she knows that. Like I said, she's a very smart woman. What is this Rice research she talked about?"

"I don't know," I answer. But you better believe it's getting Googled when I get home.

"She won't leave you alone now. Especially with the website back up and running. She sees you as a threat. You should change your appearance so she won't be able to find you as easily. I'd be happy to give you some money if you need it..."

"No, I've got it covered."

"I could provide a security guard or two..."

Someone following me around, watching everything I do? Uh, no thank you. What would the Griz think if I had two strange people following me around? Then I'd have to tell her about all of this and there's no way I'm doing that. She'd never let me leave the house again. Fiona would have to blow it up to get rid of me.

"No, thank you. I'll be all right."

It's a struggle for him in that suit and those shoes, but he stands and I follow his lead.

"You deserve her," he says and holds his hand out to me to shake.

"Who?" I ask.

"Lexi."

I don't believe him, but I smile anyway. I thought finding out about Alexis would help me fit into this body better, but the more I learn about her, the more I'm convinced I don't belong in here. She woke up in the morning and worried about whose life she was going to save that day. I wake up in the morning and worry about accidentally touching peanuts.

"Can you do me a favor?" I ask.

"Sure."

"Don't put cream in your coffee anymore." I only just met this man, but I liked him instantly. Fiona's threat worries me.

He doesn't take her threat as seriously as I do and laughs. "Don't worry, I won't. Don't forget I'm on the inside. If you need anything I can get for you, I'll try my hardest. I'll keep an eye on Fiona and keep searching for something, anything we can use to prove that she's the one responsible. Here's my card. Don't call the number on the front. It's my work phone. It shouldn't be monitored, but at this point I wouldn't put it past her. Like I said, she's smart." He reaches into an inside pocket and pulls out a pen. Then he scribbles something on the back of the card and hands it to me. "Call the number on the back if you need to talk. It's a burner cell. They can't track it. It's what I use to communicate with the private investigators I've hired. I'll help you any way I can. And hey – I wouldn't come out here again at night. If I could find you, she can find you."

He's right.

Now I'll never make the track team.

* * *

I don't get back into the house until after midnight and even when the head sinks into the pillow, I can't fall asleep. The glow-in-the-dark galaxy on my ceiling is almost faded. I usually try to get to sleep before they fade to nothing.

They remind me of my dad because he put them there. They're not cheesy looking five pointed stars that come in a package from the grocery store. I have an actual replica of the sky on my ceiling. I guess that's what you get when your dad is an astronomer. Was an astronomer.

Since he died I've pictured him as the M75 cluster. Sagittarius was his favorite constellation. It's kind of comforting to look up at your dad and see him looking down on you before you fall asleep.

But tonight the star version of him doesn't comfort me. Why does everything seem so much more terrifying in the middle of the night with the lights off? When the only sounds you hear are the scary creaks and the train whistles?

I'm scared for Jaz. The lupus is one thing, but what if what I've done is so much worse? What if Fiona comes after her like she came after me? Not only did I plaster Jaz all over the website, I wheeled her directly to Fiona. Jaz is defenseless. I could never forgive myself if anything happened to her.

18

The Feet Don't Dance

I'm a block away from my house walking home from school when I get a text from Jaz asking if I can stop by the hospital tonight. She doesn't say why and I don't ask. Jaz needs me, that's it. No questions needed.

Mom's not so easy to convince since she just dropped me off there yesterday after school.

"It can't be healthy to spend so much time at a hospital, Nessa. There are so many sick people there. Once a week, I don't have a problem with that. But every day? Is there something going on I should know about?" Mom holds a pile of stiff spaghetti noodles in her hands and breaks them all in half before dumping them in a pot of boiling water.

"It's not everyday, Mom. Just today. And I'm sure it's nothing serious. I think Jaz just gets lonely. She's one of the oldest kids on the unit and she didn't look good at all yesterday. I'm really worried about her. She's really sick this time, Mom. Can you not be the Griz for one night and let me take her some jelly beans?"

She sighs loudly and sticks the wooden spoon in the pan of tomato sauce. "Alright, but it's your last time there this week. I'm not a huge fan of hanging out in the hospital lobby."

* * *

The hospital parking lot is full. Not with cars, but with news vans with big letters and numbers on the sides and huge antennas and dishes on top.

They're here for Jaz!

Her story went live on the blog last night and Cole sent out a ton of press releases to every media outlet he could think of. My stomach is flip flopping like it's full of fish when Mom finally pulls into an empty parking spot at

146

the end of the lot and we begin our long hike to the main entrance.

She's busy trying to determine what celebrity might be here but I only half-listen to her.

My smile is so wide, the corners of my lips tickle my ears. I don't tell her, but I know who the celebrity is. My blue-haired friend, Jaz. The bravest girl I know.

There are no reporters in the lobby, none by the gift shop, and I don't see any on my way to the elevator. They're crazy if they think they're all going to fit into Jaz's small room. Her mom will freak.

I've taken this elevator up hundreds of times but this time is different. I hear something I've never heard before the closer it gets to the third floor. The elevator vibrates with rhythmic bumping of loud music and suddenly I'm confused. Don't reporters have a microphone and ask people questions? Why would they want to play music?

The door opens to reveal a party. A giant party. The hallway is filled with balloons, flying confetti, and sick kids dancing in the hallways to one of the latest pop hits. And in the middle of it is Jaz, facing the elevator, holding onto her wheelie, the only person here without joy on her face. I stand rooted to the floor of the elevator, confusion stopping my ability to take a step out of it.

The door starts to close automatically, finally triggering the hand to reach out and stop it.

"I'm so glad — you made it!" Jaz exclaims when I reach her. "I just couldn't —handle..."

"VANESSA!" Her voice pierces through the screams, through the feet pounding the floor, through the music being pumped out of giant speakers by a DJ next to the nurses station.

Fiona Gray.

She glides through the dancing kids like she's on skates, but she's not. She's wearing those leopard-printed high-heeled shoes again, this time with a grey, tailored suit. Her arms are held out as she walks up to me and uses them to embrace me in a hug. I stand stiff and don't hug her back. No way. Only when I'm looking around her do I notice the news cameras, recording every movement she makes.

"You will never win this," she whispers in the left ear.

"What is this?" I ask.

"It's a party, silly!" She doubles over in fake laughter and turns around to join the rest of the dancing kids. "DJ! Can you cut the music for a minute?"

She grabs the handles of a nearby wheelchair with a small boy inside and wheels him in front of the nurse's station.

"Jasmine, will you join us up here?" she yells our way.

Jaz shakes her head, no.

"Fine, you then! Come up here with me!" She points to a girl who might be ten and is trying to balance on crutches. She happily makes her way through the crowd of kids to stand at Fiona's side.

The camera men line up in front.

"As you probably know, I'm Fiona Gray, and I invented L.E.A.M., the cure for lupus. I'm here to let you all know that I'm working *very* hard to come up with cures for *all* of your ailments!"

The crowd of kids, most of them now sitting on the floor in front of her, cheer loudly.

Jaz looks at me with a smirk and an eye roll. I hand her the bag of jelly beans I brought. Anything to keep my mind off of the evil woman standing in front of us.

"There's nothing I love more in this world than children which is why I'm here to present a check to the hospital for one hundred thousand dollars to set up a new technology center that you'll all be able to use whenever you feel well enough!"

More cheers. Loud applause. From the kids, from the nurses, one of the reporters even tucks her microphone under her arm so she can clap.

"She wants everyone — to think she's a Saint," Jaz says.

"And a little bird told me that you all love stuffed animals, so I bought what I could at the toy store. If I bought too many you can all have a few!"

Two men come out from behind the nurse's station with large bags and start passing out perfect-looking machine-sewn teddy bears, lions, penguins, giraffes, and every other stuffed animal you could think of. Some kids don't have enough arm room to hold them all.

"Oh, Nessa!" Jaz's face has fallen into a frown when she looks at me. "They're total crap — you know that, right? I don't see any — with horns. Well, except — maybe that goat. I wouldn't have — told you to come — if I would have known…"

150

"It's alright." But it isn't. None of this is alright and I try really hard to fight back tears. Fiona isn't a wonderful person. She doesn't love children. She's using her money to try to make herself look good and take the focus off of Jaz and her feature on Alexis's website. And she didn't professionally hand sew any of these animals!

We retreat to Jaz's room when the music blares again and I feel like I'm going to throw up. I just want to go home and crawl into bed. What kid is going to want my monsters when they have an entire zoo of top-quality stuffed animals from Fiona?

We close the door behind us, but it's not thick enough to block out the sounds of the party on the other side.

"I thought the reporters were here for you," I say when she's situated back in her bed.

"They were. I was in the middle — of an interview when Fiona showed up — and pulled them out, saying she had a bigger — human interest story for them."

I groan.

Jaz falls asleep and the music stops within a half-hour. I open her door a crack to make sure Fiona's gone. I don't want to see her. Not now, not ever again.

The DJ is tearing down his equipment and the janitor is sweeping up the confetti. All of the kids have returned to their rooms, probably to snuggle with their new stuffed and furry best friends. I don't see Fiona. I think it's safe.

I'm almost to the elevator when one of the nurses calls my name.

It's the same nurse that gave me the money a few days ago.

"Ms. Gray left this for you. She's *such* a sweet woman." I nod, but that nod is a lie. There's nothing sweet about Fiona. She puts an envelope in my hand with my name written on the front. It's a good thing I'm in a hospital in case there's peanut residue inside. I open it cautiously, half expecting something to jump out at me, but it's just a notecard with three words written on it.

Research for safety.

19

The Hair Becomes Blonde

The envelope of monster donation money had $465 inside.

Enough money to fund my transformation.

The hair cut to the shoulders and dye to platinum blond used $150 of it. A hair straightener took another $100. Twin and I picked out makeup at the drugstore and some non-prescription glasses for another $50. The rest I spent on new clothes. Clothes I wouldn't have been caught dead in before, but am wearing now.

I did *not* get them from Trendz.

Last night I thought it would be fun to count how many people don't recognize me today when I walk down the hallway at school, but I've already lost count and I'm not to the common area yet. It would be easier to count the people who do recognize me.

Two. Twin and Cole.

I had the woman doing my hair give me a bright turquoise streak right in front. Partly to represent the rebellious person I need to be and partly for Jaz.

We'll match and she'll love it.

"You ready for this?" Twin asks. I nod. "Man, I'd pay good money to be there when Carly sees you."

I'm ready, but I'm not looking forward to it. I'm smart enough to know that nothing there is going to change. She still hates me and is still going to make fun of me no matter what I look like. But I know now the only thing I can change is how I react.

Carly's days of winning are over.

* * *

Mom kind of freaked out when she saw the new Nessa.

The glasses didn't bother her as much as the hair and the new clothes did. She asked me if I was having an identity crisis and I told her it's been going on for a year now and it was a major parent fail if she was just now noticing it.

154

After that she let it drop. Until today.

"I got a call from the corporate office this morning telling me they need me in San Francisco tomorrow." She lays the tater-tot casserole down in the middle of the dining room table and hands me the giant spoon so I can scoop mine out first. "I almost told them 'no' at the risk of losing my job."

"Why would you tell them no?" I ask between chews. She loves to travel for work. It's usually only a few days and she says it helps clear her head.

"Because of you, Nessa! Because I'm starting to wonder if I even know who you are. I don't recognize you! You think you've been poisoned and doctors that don't exist tell you that you haven't, a weird woman shows up and gets dragged out of our front yard, and I know you sneak out of the house when I go to bed! I checked on you Monday night. You weren't in your bed or anywhere else in this house. Where did you go?"

No way!

I forgot about the woman in the front yard. She recognized this body as Alexis O'Riley's before *I* knew it belonged to Alexis O'Riley. She was so upset, I'd bet anything she is either on the list of Alexis's contacts or knows someone who is.

155

"Um — Va-nessa?" The split syllables of my name means the Griz is on her way for a visit. Not someone I really want to deal with right now. "Are you going to answer my question? Where did you go Monday night?"

The head feels like it splits in half when she yells. I put both hands over both ears.

"I went to the track behind school to practice."

"You're kidding me, right? You can't do that when it's daylight?"

"No," I say and shove another huge bite of the casserole in the mouth hoping she'll see it's full and that I can't answer any of her questions.

"Why not? And don't worry," she looks at the mouth with disgust, "I can wait."

I've never chewed a mouthful of food for so long in my entire life. I'm not wasting time. I'm trying to think of a good answer to her question, but I can't. The only answer I can think of is the truth and I can barely admit it to myself, much less tell it to my mother.

"Well?" she asks as I finally swallow it down in one huge gulp.

"What do you think the other kids will say when they see the fat girl trying to run the track? Let's just say I've heard enough fat jokes to last me a lifetime and I've only had this body for a year. And Dad's out there at night. I can lay on the track and see Sagittarius with no trees blocking my view."

"You're not fat, Nessa. You just weigh a little more than you used to. You used to be so thin, a few extra pounds would actually be a good thing."

"Twenty pounds is not a few," I say.

"You have bigger bones," she says as she grabs the giant spoon and dives it in for another scoop.

"Fabulous. Just what I always wanted. Bigger bones."

"Believe it or not, I don't care about your bones. That's not what we were talking about. Do you know how dangerous it is to walk there by yourself at night? Someone could be hiding under the bleachers or..."

"I know, Mom." Believe me, I know. I have Mr. O'Riley to thank for that lesson. "I won't ever do it again. Pinky swear. Even if they're hers." I hold the littlest finger up and wiggle it.

"You're staying at Twin's house until I get back. Corporate said I should only have to be there a few days."

"Fine."

"McKenna said you can use Anna's room." Anna is Twin's older sister who's at college.

157

"Are we done?" I ask.

"You'll have to get packed up tonight and I'll drop your things off at McKenna's on the way to the airport. You'll need to go home with Twin tomorrow after school, my flight leaves at 2 in the afternoon. No tripping on big rocks on the way home from school or anything, if that's what *really* happened."

The Griz smiles and I know I'm forgiven.

For now.

20

The Eyes Read the Police Report

"Oh. My. God." Carly stops in the middle of the doorway to our French class and at least three kids behind crash into her. "Did you get *another* body?"

I smile at her sweetly.

She saunters in, long blond hair swinging across her back, and sits in the desk behind me. Any other day she sits on the other side of the room, as far away from me as she can get. She smells like too much perfume and I fight back the urge to gag.

"So — I'm dying to know. Did that second body reject you, too? Your brain must be like a parasite. Maybe you should have them put it under the microscope in biology and see what's wrong."

As much as I'd love to remind her of the chocolate pudding incident in the cafeteria, I don't. Cole won that battle for me and I have to be able to do it myself.

"This is the same body, Carly. I just got tired of the red friz. You should've seen me try to run a brush through it every morning. How's Mark doing? I haven't seen him forever. Is he in the fourth grade this year?"

I had a strategy for today. Talk to her like I did when we were friends. Pretend she never got mean. Pretend we never left her cafeteria table and that she hasn't been who she's been for the past year. Mark is her little brother and her weakness. She may hate the rest of the world, but she loves Mark.

"He's — good." She stutters.

"Please tell him I said 'hey' next time you see him, okay?"

She doesn't answer. Instead she stands up and heads to the other side of the room where she normally sits.

Mrs. Beatty yells at her for getting up after class has started, but Carly ignores her.

I'm sure she's back there coming up with something nasty to say to me at lunch, but I don't care anymore.

Carly's the least of my problems.

* * *

"Are you *trying* to get me arrested?" Cole asks in between bites of hash brown.

"It's the quickest way I can think of to get you to stop sitting with me at lunch, so yeah. Do you think you can get it?" I ask. Of course, I'm joking. I'm almost as comfortable around Cole as I am with Twin or Jaz now. He's been calling every night, telling me about the website and giving me the internet traffic stats.

"You know, *you* could get it by walking through the doors of the police department and asking the person at the front desk for a copy of the police report. It's public record. Then I wouldn't be breaking hundreds of laws by trying to hack into the police department's records."

"I don't have a way to get there." I pull an apple from my brown paper bag and sink the teeth into it.

Being fourteen really sucks when you have important things to accomplish that involve driving. I don't want to get Cole in trouble, but I really need to find out who the woman was in my front yard.

"Forget it," I say. "I think I have another way."

Mr. O'Riley only said a few words when I ducked into an empty bathroom after lunch and called him on his secret burner phone. He was probably at work. I told him the date the woman was pulled out of my front yard and asked him if he could get me a copy of the police report. He answered with a few 'yes's and a few 'uh-huh's and quickly hung up.

* * *

"So what do you want to do first? We can pop popcorn and watch movies, or see if Mom will take us shopping," Twin is way too excited about me staying at her house for a few days. I look for the big rock on the sidewalk, but don't see it anywhere. Someone must've kicked it into the woods.

I don't tell her that I packed my laptop and plan to spend my time there researching the names on Alexis's list of L.E.A.M. patients.

I see Toby poking his head out behind one of the trees before Twin does. She's too busy yapping about new nail polish colors and the selfies we're going to take.

This time he looks at me weird when I smile at him, then he smiles back.

"Twin," I interrupt her. "Toby's over in the woods. I have to go talk to him for a minute."

She does a full, abrupt stop and stares at me.

"You've got to be kidding me."

I shake my head, no. "You're welcome to come with me, if you want."

"If I *want*? Do I have a choice?" She follows close behind, and stomps every step to make sure I know she doesn't want to like she's three-years-old.

"I almost didn't know you were you," he says as we walk into the woods for a few minutes. The further we are from the road, the safer we are. I hope. "You don't look like Alexis anymore."

"Yeah, that's kind of the point."

He doesn't say anything for about a minute and I wonder if he's sad that I don't look like her or if he's just trying to process the information. I'm actually glad. I didn't want him looking at me and thinking I'm still his sister. When the 'me' is just my brain.

He stops walking and sits on a rock big enough to hold him. There's nothing for me to sit on, so I lean against a nearby tree and Twin moves her foot around in the leaves next to me, pretending not to listen.

"Here, Dad said you needed this."

I take it from him but shove it into my bag without opening it. I'll look at it when I get to Twin's. In private.

"Thanks. You're fast."

"We release a half hour before Johnny Appleseed does. Gave me plenty of time to drive to the police department, then here. I saw her website featured on the news this morning before I left for school. Looks like what you're doing is working."

Twin's head shoots up and she glares at me.

I haven't turned on the TV since Jaz's information went live. The only time I can watch it is when I'm at home and there's no way I want the Griz to see Jaz's picture plastered all over the news. She'll ask questions that I don't want to answer. If I don't turn it on, then I'm safe. Mom never watches TV. She says the only information she needs is in books.

"I hope I'm doing the right thing," I say.

"You're not," Twin mumbles only loud enough for me to hear.

"After I saw it," Toby says, "I couldn't help thinking about how happy Alexis would be right now. Then I got a panicked text from Meg. She's afraid they'll think it was her that put it up. Let's just say you're not at the top of her favorite list."

I laugh, nervously. When I published that post I was only thinking about Jaz and what she wanted. Hoping somehow this would help her. I never thought about how it would impact anyone else or put them in danger.

"Tell her she doesn't have to worry. They know it's me for sure," I say.

"Nessa," Twin interrupts. "I forgot to tell you that my mom was planning to have dinner early. We really have to get going."

I look at Twin and know she's lying. I can always tell. She takes the front lock of hair that always falls over her face, shoves it behind her ear then plays with it. Like she's doing now.

"Thanks, Toby. I really appreciate this," I say.

"Can I give you girls a ride home? Probably safer than walking."

"Are you going to offer us candy, too?" Twin snaps. "No thanks, we'll walk." She grabs my wrist and pulls me back through the woods, toward the street.

I can only imagine how red the face must be right now.

* * *

The crying lady in my front yard was Mary Rice. Her address on the police report is in Muncie, Indiana. Two and a half hours away. I know, I mapped it on my phone. I have no idea what made me forget what Fiona said in the elevator, but now I remember she said "Rice's research" which was probably Dr. Seymour Rice, the researcher who died the day before Alexis. There was a news article about his death on Alexis's disk.

And I'd bet a hundred dollars that he's somehow related to Mary Rice, the crying woman at my front door.

There's a knock on the bathroom door. It's so sudden, it rips me from my thoughts and makes the body jump.

"You about done in there?" Twin pounds on the door again, harder this time. "You've been in there for like twenty minutes."

But all I hear her say is "Blah, blah, blah." My brain is filled with thoughts of Mary Rice. She drove two and a half hours to knock on my door? And then left wailing in police custody. Who does that unless they have a really good reason to?

"Are you listening to me, Nessa?"

"Yeah," I say, but I'm not.

I can't call Mary Rice. I don't *think* that my phone is being monitored, but I wouldn't be surprised if hers was. Especially if Fiona Gray killed her husband.

I need to find a way to get to Muncie, Indiana.

With Twin and her mother, the Griz-in-training McKenna Sanders, that's not going to be easy.

21

The Body Tracks Down the Not-Crying-Anymore Woman

How sad is it that I feel more at home in the hospital than I do anywhere else? Home has the Griz who isn't happy unless she's sitting on me to make sure I do what she wants. And school has Carly who is still set on making my life miserable. This morning she stuck a fresh piece of chewed-up gum on my chair in French class. I got to walk around school for the rest of the day with her saliva and the goo I couldn't get off on the right back pocket of my jeans. I don't have to be a genius to know it was her. Her giggles in the back of the room once I sat down told me all I needed to know.

Jaz and I walk side-by-side down the hallway. When I walked into her room, she pulled an oxygen tube out of her nose. Jaz on oxygen was new and scary. I know it's been harder for her to talk lately but — her being hooked up to a tube in her nose just scares me.

Twin and Cole should both be here by now. We turn the corner by the nurse's desk and see them sitting in the common area.

"Are you nervous?" I ask because her voice had that panicked tone to it where all of her words were really short because they came out so fast. That and she flips the hair on her wig every few seconds.

"No, but why would Cole — want to meet me?"

"He's the one that's been feeding your information to the press. He said his life won't be complete until he meets you. Well, that and I've been lying non-stop telling him all of this fake, wonderful stuff about you."

"I have a feeling that I'm not — the person he thinks — will make his life complete."

"I have no idea what you mean," I tell her with cheeks that feel warmer than bread fresh out of the oven.

"You're taller than — Nessa said you were," Jaz says to Cole once we reach the common room. She parks her wheelie and sits next to him on the couch.

"Nessa told you what I look like?" I glance at Cole and his wink makes me want to run back down to the lobby and call McKenna to come and take me back to their house. Twin gives a little wave and sits in a chair across from them, like I do.

"How are you handling all of your sudden fame?" Twin asks Jaz. They've met before, when Twin would visit after my surgery.

"Honestly?" Jaz looks at me, almost like she's afraid to give an honest answer because I'll hear. "I hate it. I've never liked — being in the spotlight. And now everyone — wants to talk to me. Except the people at BioMed, of course."

Twin called this 'meeting' and made sure the three of us took extra precautions when we arrived so no one would notice we were all arriving together. I'll give it to her, she's thorough. She had Cole hack into the hospital's patient database right after school and get them random names to ask for at the front desk. McKenna dropped us off a half-hour ago. She dropped me off first and ran Twin back home when she faked an "I forgot my phone and I really

170

need it to show Nessa's friend Jaz something." Cole just got here. His dad dropped him off but not before asking, "Is this where kids are hanging out these days?" Cole just told him 'yes' to keep him from asking any more questions.

I have no idea what we're going to talk about, but I have a feeling Twin is finally trying to get more involved. She asked a lot of questions on the way home from seeing Toby in the woods and didn't get mad when I answered them.

"Well," she says, "This is actually more of an intervention than a meeting. Vanessa, we all love you, but you can't update that website again." I look at Jaz and Cole who both look shocked. "These people are trying to kill you! And you're taking it and shoving it in their faces. How do you think that's going to end up? With you alive? Ha! I don't think so. I called us all together so we can talk you out of this."

The tongue is numb. It wouldn't move if I wanted it to. Maybe I knew this was coming, but it didn't make me any more prepared.

"I'm not talking her out of anything," Cole speaks up.

"Me neither," Jaz agrees. "Nessa is smart enough to make — her own decisions."

171

The four of us go silent as a nurse pushes her laptop cart through the hallway behind us. Twin picks up her tablet and moves her finger across the screen, pretending to be busy on it.

It's clear the four of us know we can't trust anyone.

"Do you know she's been in contact with Mr. O'Riley? Alexis's dad? Not only is it dangerous seeing as how he works for BioMed, but according to the details of her *closed* transplant, it's completely illegal!"

I'm still in shock. I knew Twin wasn't happy that I was getting involved in all of this, but I never thought she'd pull my friends together and try to turn them against me.

"Is that true?" Cole asks me.

I tell them how I met Alexis's dad at the track that night and how we both believe Fiona Gray is the one behind all of this. But only Jaz has seen the real Fiona. To Twin and Cole she's just a name. They have no idea how terrifying she really is.

"Vanessa!" Twin yells my name louder than anyone should talk in a hospital. "You can't trust him. Of all people in this world, you can't trust that man! He works for BioMed. Of course he would try to put the blame on someone else!" She looks frantically to the others. "Am I the only one who can see this?"

"You think I don't know who he works for?" I argue. "You think he would kill his *daughter*? He wants to find out who and why just as much as we do. And he's on the inside. He can get us any information we need. I asked him for the police report and he had it hand-delivered to me in *hours*. I have a gut feeling. We can trust him."

"It's not your gut feeling, Nessa. Not when it's *her* gut about *her* dad. I will never trust him. He's the enemy." Twin stands up and stomps her foot in anger. "I can't believe you're too blind to see that. If you're being this reckless with your life then I'm not going to help you. I have tons of better things I could be doing right now."

"Like what?" Cole asks.

Twin's lips purse together as she struggles to find an answer.

Anger brings me to the feet and my words come out so fast and fierce, I don't get to think them over first. The skin is on fire from the tips of the toes to the hair follicles on the head.

"You were the one who wanted me to like this body! You wanted me to get used to it so I'd quit complaining to you about it. Well, learning more about Alexis is helping me do that. Isn't that what you wanted? Now you've changed your mind? What happened to supporting your best friend no matter what happens, just because she's your best friend and you love her?"

"I can't watch you get hurt again! It was hard enough thinking I'd lost you the first time." She slams her butt back down in the chair.

"If Nessa trusts Alexis's dad then — she must have a good reason other — than her stomach. I believe in what Nessa — is trying to do. He may be able to help us, and right now — we need all the help we can get. We'll just have to — be careful around him. Until we know for sure. No meeting with him — or Toby alone. Someone should be — with Nessa at all times." Jaz looks at me with a smile on her face, and Twin looks at me with anger on hers.

I walk Jaz back to her room when Cole leaves. Twin texts her mom to pick us up and goes to the lobby to wait for her. She's mad that her 'intervention' didn't go the way she wanted it to, but there's nothing I can do about that. I'm not apologizing. I don't have time for drama. But most of all, I'm hurt. It's always been Twin and I against the world. And what are we now? Against each other? I don't know how to live like that. I don't *want* to live like that.

"Thanks for defending me back there," I tell Jaz.

"You don't owe me — thanks for anything. It's me who owes you. I know you're — doing all of this for me. I just hope that you trust — Mr. O'Riley for the right reason."

"Is there a wrong reason?"

"He was Alexis's dad. He'll never be yours."

Ouch. I stop pushing the wheelie and stand rooted to the floor in the middle of the hospital hallway.

"I never said..." I mumble.

"I know you didn't. I'm just scared about you — getting too involved with anyone — from her life. Lines can get blurred when — they look at you and see everything — they've always seen in her."

* * *

It doesn't take me long to realize that Jaz is right.

If I'm going to be around these people Alexis used to know and love, I need to be smart about it. I can't get too close. And I have to make sure they realize it's me in this body, not her.

But I also have to get to Muncie, Indiana.

In a car.

"You're not going to be happy until you see me rotting somewhere even if it's detention, are you?" Cole

175

asks when I step into the trees by school where we agreed to meet. I wrap the arms tighter around the chest, hoping it will warm me up a little. The morning air is a brisk, snappy cold. Enough to remind me that it's still spring in Ohio. I only wore a sweatshirt because I didn't want to wear a jacket and get too hot in a car for the two-and-a-half-hour drive. Now I'm second-guessing myself and I wonder if I should've brought one. I'm not a fan of being cold.

Cole wears a dark oversized sweatshirt and has the hood pulled over his head.

"Thanks so much for doing this," I say.

"You think I'm the kind of guy who would let you ride alone in a car with someone you barely know for 150 miles? Plus, Jaz made a rule and she's not someone I want to mess with."

No, I don't think he's that kind of guy. That's why I asked him to skip school on a Friday and come with me. It took every ounce of courage I could come up with to ask him. For once I couldn't rely on Twin to do it for me. I wish I could, but she's been giving me the silent treatment since we left the hospital yesterday. I had to decide not to tell her I was doing this today. I didn't want her to tell McKenna or one of the teachers. We don't share any classes, only see each other in the hallway every once in a while. I plan on acting like we just managed to miss running into each other today. She'd probably ignore me anyway. Twin doesn't like Mr. O'Riley and I can't imagine she likes Toby much either. Not telling her I'm doing this today seems like the best option. I'll tell her about it once I'm home. Maybe. Depending on how things go.

Cole already hacked into the school's computer system and marked our absences excused for today. They don't place a follow-up call to your parents if they've already gotten an excuse. He also hacked into Toby's school and fixed his attendance.

"Hey! Hop in."

A black car stops next to the sidewalk with Toby behind the wheel. Cole leans over and whispers in my ear.

"Jeez, that's like a $50,000 car. Do you want me to sit in the front seat so you won't have to?"

I nod. It's another check box to add to my thank-Cole-for list. It never occurred to me until he said it how uncomfortable and awkward it might be to sit in the front seat next to Toby considering how close he was with his sister. But it would probably be just as uncomfortable and awkward if I sat in the backseat next to Cole. I like to think I'm pretty cool around him lately, but I know I'm not. This girl could say a lot of stupid stuff to a boy in two-and-a-half hours.

I climb into the empty back seat and shove aside a beautifully wrapped gift. It's covered in black and silver metallic striped wrapping paper with a giant silver ribbon tied in a bow on top. I've seen tons of presents in my lifetime, but I've never seen one wrapped this perfectly. The folds are straighter than straight and you can't even see the tape holding it together.

I love presents. Who doesn't? But after the chat I had with Jaz last night on the way back to her room, I really hope this one isn't for me.

I snap my belt into place and thank Toby for skipping school to do this.

"Hey, that gift in the back is from our — I mean, my dad."

My dad used to get me presents. For all of my birthdays and holidays Mom bought all of my gifts, but he would get me a special one just from him. Christmas was rough this year without it. My birthday was worse because it was right after we lost him. I've often wondered if it would get easier as time goes on. So far it hasn't.

Right now the perfect present on the other seat makes my heart hurt when I'm sure Mr. O'Riley thought he was doing a good thing. I can't do this.

"Can you pull over?" I ask.

"What?" Both Toby and Cole say it together like they're twins doing some creepy say-what-the-other-one-is-saying thing.

"Please, I'll only be a second."

Toby slows the car down and stops it in a doctor's office parking lot.

"Pop the trunk?" I ask.

I don't waste any time. We don't have a lot to spare if we're going to get to Muncie and back in time for me to walk home from school with Twin like I was never gone. The box isn't too heavy. I've got it in the empty trunk of the car and am back, belted in my seat in less than a minute.

"I'm not going to ask," Cole says, leaning around the front passenger seat to look at me.

"Good."

It's a long drive, but we don't talk much. We really don't have a lot in common with Toby except this body I'm in. He's older and in high school. Cole asks him a few questions about that, but Toby gives him short answers like he'd rather concentrate on driving than answering. After a while, Cole gives up trying to make conversation.

I'm not listening to them, anyway. I'm busy figuring out what to say to Mary Rice when I knock on her door at 4351 Deer Run Drive. She knows me as Alexis O'Riley, but I'm not going to knock on her door and introduce myself as Alexis. Could I introduce myself as the girl who ended up in Alexis O'Riley's body? Maybe if I want her to slam the door closed in my face. Which I don't. I shed the Alexis look with my makeover; she may not even recognize me now.

I think I'll just start by telling her I knew she was in my front yard a few weeks ago and I'd like to talk to her.

It's the least weird option.

I just hope it works and I'm not the one being carried off of *her* front yard by the police this time.

22

The Eyes See the Time

It works.

Mary Rice's eyes bug out of her face, then she looks nervously down the cul-de-sac.

"Were you followed?" she asks.

"No," Toby answers. "I kept checking behind us to make sure." I have no idea if that's the truth or if he just said it because he sees how freaked out she is. I didn't even think to check for someone following us.

She pulls us into the large house and slams the door before I have a chance to object. I'm not sure being in this woman's house is the smartest place to be right now. I don't even know for sure who she is. I feel a little safer knowing

Toby and Cole are with me, but still. I'm not following her down to the dark basement or anything.

She leaves us in the hall without a word and disappears.

Toby turns to us and grips the doorknob to the front door.

"Can we go now?" he whispers.

And instantly she's back.

"Just had to close some blinds. I'm sure they watch." She says in a tone slightly louder than a whisper.

"Who is 'they'?" Cole asks.

Instead of answering, her eyes get wide and she taps an ear with her index finger. Cole snaps his head so he's facing me and his eyes get wide. I can't tell if she's amusing or scaring him. I'm mostly scared. This isn't the first time I've dealt with her and the last time wasn't a whole lot better.

"Follow me," she says and walks away from us into a bigger room. The three of us look at each other. I'm not going first. It's going to have to be one of them. Cole rolls his eyes and takes off after her.

"Ladies first," Toby swings his arm out after them.

"Do I have to?" I ask, but I put the freckled jelly legs in motion and in a few steps enter the giant room with a tall ceiling.

The outside of the house was gorgeous when we walked up to the door. Brick, well-kept, and huge. You could fit five of my houses inside of this one. But inside, well, it's the complete opposite. There's hardly any furniture and the walls look like someone put a sledgehammer through them and pulled wires out. *Through the walls.* There are big holes with lines behind them. They almost look like balloon holes. I count seven of them, a few on each wall.

And the *smell.* I've never smelled anything like it before, so I have nothing to compare it to, but it sure isn't pleasant. It makes me want to run back to the car, roll down all the windows and wait there while Toby and Cole find out what we came here for.

"You're *her,* aren't you?" she says. "The green eyes."

"Well," I don't know how to explain this to her. I have a suspicion that sanity may have left her a while ago.

"Alexis O'Riley died," Toby says, coming to my rescue. "When she did, they transplanted Vanessa's brain into Alexis's body. So this is really Vanessa. In Alexis O'Riley's body."

"Oh," she stares at me like she's looking for proof of my brain behind my eyes. "Yes, yes. I understand."

She does? Just like that? I still don't understand and I've been living like this for almost a year.

"Have a seat and we can talk." The three of us look around. There's nothing to sit on. She falls to the floor and folds her legs in front of her. "It's safe to talk here. There were bugs but I got rid of them." She points to one of the balloon shapes in the wall.

Cole's panicked look makes me want to laugh but I don't dare. This woman ripped wires out of her walls with her bare hands. I'm not going to be the one to upset her.

I fall to the floor in front of her and the boys follow my lead.

"Is your husband Dr. Seymour Rice?" Cole asks.

"Was."

She offers no more information.

"We found an article about his death in Alexis's things. How did you know her?" I ask, hoping she'll say more. Maybe she just needs to be asked the right question.

"Seymour contacted her. He'd been working on a natural cure for lupus for years. He almost had it figured out when L.E.A.M. exploded on the market, claiming to be the miracle drug with a hundred percent success rate. Because they already had a cure with L.E.A.M., he couldn't get anyone to back him financially. That didn't stop him. He did a lot of research and testing on L.E.A.M. and didn't think it would work in the long term. So he kept researching. And testing. He got hold of Alexis as soon as his testing came back positive - his cure worked! She was going to publish his research on her website as a natural alternative to L.E.A.M. Hopefully get him some exposure and a drug company to start production and trials. The day he died, he said he was driving to Columbus to give her the drive with all of his files. I remember exactly what it looked like, a thin black stick with bright blue stripes on the side."

She pauses then and stares into space for minutes. I'm beginning to think that either we'll never get the end of the story or one doesn't exist.

"And?" Toby asks.

She snaps back to reality. I actually see her pupils come into focus again.

"And I never saw Seymour again. The police knocked on my door that night saying he'd been killed in a car accident in Ohio. His car was hit hard, spun lots of times and ended up in a cornfield. I still don't know if he was on his way to her or if he had already delivered it when he was hit. But here's what I do know. Those people at BioMed killed him. They bugged our house. In the walls."

Obviously.

"What day was that?" Toby asks her.

"April 24. Did they kill her, too?" Mary asks.

"That seems to be the popular opinion," Cole says.

That was two days before my car accident, but I don't say it. No one here would care.

"The day after Seymour's accident Alexis had a severe allergy attack. Her brain never recovered, it was deprived of oxygen for too long." Toby lifts his arm and wipes it against his eyes.

"So you have no idea where the disk with Seymour's research is?" I ask.

Mary shakes her head. "At first, I wondered if they got it out of his car after they ran him off the road. But I don't think they did or they would've produced the drug by now themselves. L.E.A.M. 2.0 or something like that."

"Have you ever heard the name Fiona Gray?" I ask.

"Ha!" Mary's laugh is so loud, the empty walls vibrate with it. "Do I know Fiona Gray? She offered to buy Seymour's research, but only if he would release all copyright to it. Do you know how much L.E.A.M. costs? So much that medical insurances won't cover it. The only people who get 'cured' with L.E.A.M. are the people who can afford to pay for it. Because Fiona Gray owns the copyright and won't release it to anyone other than BioMed who pays her to produce it. But what about everyone else? If you're too poor to buy L.E.A.M. and fill Fiona Gray's pockets with cash, then too bad. You'll be sick for the rest of your life until you die. Seymour didn't want that. He wanted everyone to have the information for his cure for free. If more manufacturers make it, the cost for it would be much lower and everyone could have access to it. You wouldn't have to be rich to be cured."

"Did he have a backup of the files he was giving to Alexis?" Cole asks.

"I've looked everywhere. On all the drives and disks we have, on his hard drive, even on his work computer. I've spent a year looking and have found nothing. Would you like a sardine pie? I've got one in the oven. It's got a load of vitamin B12 in it. Very healthy." Mary rubs her hands together and licks her lips.

Sardine Pie? *Gross!*

That's what the smell is. I don't care how healthy they are, I'm not going to eat a sardine. Especially baked in a pie. I want to run out of here as fast as I can, but I have two more questions for Mary.

"Why did you come to my house and ask for Alexis and how did you know what she looked like?"

"She had texted Seymour a picture of herself so he'd recognize her when they met. He showed it to me before he left. It's still on his phone that they recovered from the accident. I'm not sure where they were meeting, he never said if he was driving all the way to Columbus or if they were meeting somewhere in between. There's nothing about that on his phone. Then I saw you on the news, and knew you were her even though you gave that reporter a different name. I called close to a hundred 'Meadows' in the Columbus phone directory before your mother answered and told me I could talk to you. I loved Seymour. He worked so hard on this, I just don't want to see what he did wasted or in Fiona Gray's hands so she can take credit for it. I don't want him to have died for nothing. If you can find those files, I want you to publish them. That's all he ever wanted."

* * *

188

"Were Seymour's files on that disk Meg gave you?" Toby asks. He hits a button on his steering wheel to change the station again. Every time I get into a song he changes it.

"Unless she had the files hidden somehow, no," Cole says. "But I'll check again when I'm home just to be sure."

I can't get the smell of burnt sardines out of the nose. I think the smell attached to the little nose hairs inside. Or maybe it's my clothes. Or the hair. I hope Twin doesn't smell it on me when we walk home together. But I'm only kidding myself. Twin notices *everything*.

I look up at the wrong time. Literally.

The white numbers on the dashboard clock read 1:34 and suddenly the past year dissolves around me and I'm back where I last saw 1:34 on a car dashboard.

"Honey, I'm feeling a little tired. If I pull off at the next exit will you drive?" Dad sounds tired. He must've stayed up too late working again. He's been doing that a lot lately. It's like 1:30 in the afternoon. No one gets tired then. Well, maybe pre-schoolers.

"Sure. Anything to get you to stop driving like a maniac," Mom answers.

She's joking. Dad's the safest driver on the planet. He studies manuals at night. I haven't caught him but I have my suspicions.

"Hey! There's a Dairy Queen! Can we stop?" I jump up and down on the backseat even though I know he hates it. He says it distracts him from keeping his eyes on the road.

"We're on our way to a birthday party, Nessa. There's a hundred percent probability that there will be cake and ice cream there. And you want to stop at a Dairy Queen? STOP JUMPING LIKE THAT!" he screams.

I go stiff. Dad never yells like that. Mom and I both yell, but he's the King of Calm. Always.

I don't know how to answer him, so I don't. I turn and stare out of the window, willing the tears to stop forming. I'm used to being yelled at by Mom. She's done it so much it doesn't have much effect on me. But not Dad. I can't take it from him.

"Nessa, honey, did you try that new shampoo I got yesterday? What did you think?"

She can't think I'm that stupid. I know she's just trying to change the subject and make me forget that Dad just tore into me.

"It was glorious. Not only did it make my head feel lighter than a balloon, but I feel a million times smarter because it seeped into my head through my skin and enhanced my brain."

"Really, Vanessa." Mom sighs. "It was a simple question."

"So was mine about Dairy Queen."

Point and score.

I stare at the clock on the dashboard. 1:34. I'll die if I'm in this car with them for one more minute.

As fate would have it, I almost did.

23

My Brain Finds Its Identity

"Nessa!" I open the eyes to Cole facing me from the front seat, yelling.

"What?" Where am I?

"You were screaming. And out of it."

"We're not dead?" I ask, confused.

"Um — no. Why would we be?" Cole's tone of voice gives off the impression that I'm an idiot for asking. "Toby doesn't drive *that* bad." He laughs nervously.

We're not dead. The clock on the dashboard reads 1:37.

I survived.

We're on a stretch of old highway surrounded by cornfields on both sides. No cars in front of us, no cars behind us. I wish I could relax, but I can't. Too much has happened and my memory is still too fresh. I sit on the hands to stop them from shaking.

For almost a year I've managed to avoid being in a car at 1:34. The first month and a half was easy, I spent it in the hospital. On school days I'm still in school and on the weekends I make sure I don't go anywhere. It's gotten close a few times when Mom needed to go somewhere, but I'm a master staller. I fake sick, fake forget something or suddenly have to go to the bathroom. And it's worked until today.

Today I got distracted.

"The GPS says we'll be back in town around two. School doesn't get out until three. What are we going to do for an hour?" Cole asks Toby.

"We're going to search for Seymour's files, of course." Toby says 'of course' like he knows where the files are. But I've spent over an hour of this car ride trying to figure out where those files might be and have come up with nothing. If Alexis would have had them, she would've given them to Meg on the other disk she gave her before she died. The one we have that Cole already checked a million times.

The files aren't there.

* * *

Toby turns his car into a driveway and stops it in front of a tall iron gate. He puts the car in park and gets out. There's a screen on the stone wall at our right and his fingers fly over it like they're on auto-pilot.

On the other side the driveway turns sharply to the left with leaves and shrubbery beyond that.

"Are you sure we can trust him?" Cole asks, turning around in his seat. "Right now he's the only one who knows where we're going and we don't know what could be behind those gates. Could be a trap."

I'll never admit it to Cole or anyone else, but even I have my doubts at this point. Toby wouldn't tell us where he was taking us and that throws up a whole bag full of red flags.

"We don't have much of a choice unless you want to hop out of the car right now and make a run for it," I say. The gates begin to open from the middle, swinging in toward the greenery. Toby stands there on his phone, typing something.

"Do you want to run?" Cole asks.

"I always want to run. But I'm not doing it today."

There's something comforting about the gates. Something I can't quite figure out. It's like I've almost figured it out, to the point where I know I have the answer, but then its snatched away from me and suddenly I don't.

The drivers-side door opens and Toby climbs back in.

"I had to text Dad and tell him I'm here. He'll wonder why I'm not in school so I told him I felt sick and left."

"This is O'Riley's house?" Cole asks.

He turns around in his seat and gives me a wide-eyed-deer-caught-in-headlights look. I'm sure he's thinking what I'm thinking. Fiona Gray won't need to bother; Twin will kill us first when she finds out we were here.

That's why this place felt like home. To the body, it is.

But then the only original Nessa part of me kicks in and starts thinking of how wrong it is to bring this body back into Alexis's house without her in it. I'm an imposter. I wouldn't want some girl in *my* body going into my house or my bedroom rooting through my private stuff.

It's just wrong.

But I need to find Seymour's files. If they are everything Mary Rice says they are, it would mean that Jaz might have a chance at kicking lupus once and for all.

Not just breathe like she barely does now. She could walk, no - run out of the hospital and never have to go back. Get her real hair back instead of having to adjust the strap on her wig every time she's afraid it's going to fall off. She's never going to find the lion tamer walking through the halls of the children's wing at Columbus General.

So as wrong as it feels, I'm going into that house.

That huge house.

It looms over us as the car finishes its drive down the long driveway. There are more windows in the front of the house than monsters I've sewn in my lifetime. Well, maybe not *that* many, but it has to be close. Its stone exterior is covered with vines that weave their way around the window frames and the uneven and multicolored bricks. I count three floors. Not including a basement, if it has one.

"Did BioMed pay for this?" Cole asks Toby who answers with a nod. He stops the car and the three of us climb out.

"We don't have a lot of time if you're going to be back at school by three," Toby says. He gets out his phone and presses the screen a few times before he opens the door.

I don't stand in the tall foyer for long. The legs carry me past the ornate spiral staircase and through room after room of immaculate, expensive furniture and décor. Toby and Cole follow.

We pass an antique cabinet loaded with glassware that's probably worth more than my mom's car. It doesn't look like anyone could be comfortable in here with the shiny hardwood floors and dark curtains that block the outside light. There are no pictures. Nothing of sentimental value. The kitchen fridge is missing the notes and magnets that Mom keeps on ours and the counters look like you could lick them and not catch something. Everything is too perfect.

I open a door in the back of the kitchen and find stairs that somehow I knew would be there. The legs hop them two at a time.

Out of habit?

I pass the first landing and keep climbing to the next. It opens into a long hallway that I follow to the end.

Her door is plain. I'm not sure if I expected that or not. I've never felt more of a stranger in this body than I do right now. It knows what to expect when the hand turns the doorknob. I do not.

And I didn't think I'd see this.

Photos.

Hundreds of black and white photos plaster the walls, some poster-sized, others as small as a piece of notebook paper. They cover the walls completely. This has to be the brightest room in the house. Gauzy white curtains cover the windows letting in natural light and making the room glow.

Some people collect baseball cards. Others collect antiques or knick knacks.

Alexis collected moments.

Each photo has one captured.

I recognize some of the people. There are a few of Toby and more of Meg. Alexis even managed to get herself in a couple. I spin slowly, trying to soak in each face, each story. Each one of the photos has one.

"I think," I stop Toby's words by putting a finger to my lips. I don't want him to ruin *this* moment.

This is the real Alexis.

Alexis the storyteller.

There are a few formal, posed shots, but most of them are spontaneous. Meg laughing with a huge dark stain on the front of her shirt in the middle of a restaurant. A selfie of Alexis with the spray of Niagara Falls in the background. Toby waving at the camera from the driver's seat of the car we just pulled up in. His tongue is sticking out and his eyes are crossed. I hope that's not how he normally drives. It looks like he's holding a driver's permit in his hand.

"Did she ever *not* have her camera?" I ask him.

"I would tease her that they were going to have to surgically remove it from her hands. You wanted to know more about Alexis, these walls will tell you just about everything. You look at the photos, we'll look for the drive."

Toby and Cole set to work rummaging through her desk drawers and lifting her mattress while I soak in her memories, each caught in a single click of a button.

I laugh at the photo of Meg holding a turtle to her face. She's looking at it like she's in love. And then there's Mr. O'Riley hugging an older woman. Maybe it's Alexis's grandmother?

There are also photos of people I've never seen before, people who are sick. They have scars, dark circles under their eyes, and pale skin, but few look sad. Each one smiles like they won the life lottery. They hug family members, play with their pets, and pose next to their cars. Every smile tattoos itself on her heart and in my brain. I'm not sure I could forget any of them if I wanted to.

"She met with a lot of people who were suffering from lupus, ones that L.E.A.M. didn't provide a cure for. She offered to take their photos if they wanted her to," Toby says.

I look at each of these photos with newfound appreciation and wonder. But I also feel an overwhelming sense of pride and a feeling that I've been away from them for too long.

And there's Alexis, walking down the sandy beach alone, her hands reaching for the sky. Like there's nothing better in this world than that single moment.

Tears roll down the cheeks and I don't know why. It's a happy photo, not a sad one.

Then it hits me. Alexis appreciated every minute of her life, these walls prove it. I've never felt anything so strong. She knew who she was, full of hope and joy. Seeing her like that is catchy and instant warmth fills every bit of what used to be hers.

It feels awesome.

Alexis *lived*. In today, not yesterday or a year ago.

I've been so worried about what I lost and who I've become that I've lost sight of everything I used to love, everything I used to be. And everything I could be.

"It's not here," Cole says. I use the sleeve of my sweatshirt to wipe my face so he won't see the effect this room has had on me. But the tears won't stop coming. I can't stop them now. "Hey, you alright?" He looks at me oddly.

I nod.

Toby puts a shoebox back into her closet and checks the watch on his wrist. "Our time's up. We've got to get going if you're going to be back to school in time. I'm sorry we couldn't find it."

What he doesn't know is that I found something just as good.

I found who I am.

And it's not anyone I ever thought I would be.

24

My Hands Deliver Crookedly Sewn Monsters

I should be getting dressed for school, but I'm not.

Mr. O'Riley's gift crowds its way into my line of vision every time I look at anything else and it's driving me insane. I'm the kid that would go snooping around the closets, the attic, and the basement to find my Christmas or birthday gifts. I'm not even embarrassed that sometimes I've carefully removed the tape, unwrapped them to see what they were, then wrapped them back up again a few times. I'm stellar at faking surprise.

But this gift has been sitting on my bedroom desk for three days now and I haven't touched it. Maybe because it's wrapped too perfectly. Or maybe because I'm uncomfortable being the recipient. Whatever it is inside I don't deserve it. I'm not his daughter, I can't even remember his first name. I know it's not Mister. And I don't want him to think he should treat me like his daughter and buy me presents. You know, blurred lines and all that.

But I can't wonder about it anymore. I'll just open a corner of it and peek.

I carefully pull up the tape on one side and lift a flap of the wrapping paper. The box underneath is plain white, giving me no clue as to what's inside. Figures.

I take a deep breath and unwrap the rest. I have to be quick, if I don't I'll be late for school. The Griz returned from her trip on Friday night so she's back in full-on Nessa-needs-to-do-everything-I-say mode.

Like she heard my brain thinking about her, she yells up the stairs, asking if I'm dressed and ready for breakfast yet.

"Be down in a sec!" I yell, probably a little louder than I had to. I want to make sure she heard me. I don't need her coming up to check on me and asking who the gift is from. Why lie if I don't have to?

I pull open the top of the box to find a camera.

Alexis's camera.

I've never seen it before in my life, but I know it was hers because when I lift it out and hold it in my hands, I feel like this is the missing piece of my puzzle. The part of me that's been missing this whole time. It's weird, having something feel both old and new.

I walk to my mirror and hold the eyepiece up to my eye. I see a girl in a fuzzy white bathrobe and wet hair. Not looking anything like Vanessa Meadows and kind of looking like Alexis O'Riley.

My index finger pushes down the silver circular button.

"VA-NESSA!"

It's so loud and close that I jump and almost drop the camera.

Quicker than I think I've ever moved in my life I open my underwear drawer below and shove the camera under the clothing. I rush to my bed and kick the box and wrappings under it. Way under.

"Just couldn't decide on anything to wear today," I yell back. "I've got it, though. Almost ready!"

I quickly pull on a pair of jeans and a shirt lying on my floor. I turn in the mirror making sure there aren't any stains on them since I wore them a few days ago. The Griz would die if she knew.

But I don't plan to tell her.

There's a lot of things I don't plan to tell her.

* * *

Twin isn't waiting for me at my locker this morning. I can't say I'm surprised. We barely talked on Friday. Toby got us back to school just in time for release, but Twin wouldn't say a word to me the whole walk home. Didn't even ask why I smelled like sardine pie. I don't have to ask her why she's mad. Her 'intervention' at the hospital was an epic fail and I'm still planning to update Alexis's website. Apparently me not doing what she wants me to do means I get the silent treatment.

At dinner, she only made normal dinner conversation. "Can you pass the gravy?" or "I think I kept the butter knife" was it. Then Mom showed up to take me home.

Sure, we've had our arguments, but we've never been so mad at each other that we didn't talk. I walk up to my Twin-less locker and its emptiness stings. There's so much I want to tell her. She would love the story about the sardine pie. And Alexis's room? I want to tell her about the effect it had on me.

But I can't because she's not here.

Instead, I get Carly who must've taken an entire jar of horrible pills today. One footstep into French class and I steel myself for whatever nastiness she dishes out. She's in the back whispering to two of her friends and gets that grin on her face that means she's about to make my life miserable. Again. She's whispering to Isabelle, who is famous for giving me worst of all looks whenever she passes me in the hallway.

I take a seat in the front row, hoping she'll leave me alone if I'm close to the teacher.

But the teacher's not in the room yet leaving me open for business.

"Hey, Nessa?" She bellows sweetly from the back of the room. I don't turn around. By now I know better. "Isabelle just told me she drove past the school a few nights ago and you were running track in the dark. Trying to get skinny for Cole, maybe? You know he only talks to you because he feels sorry for you, right? I just don't want you to get your hopes up. You've had enough heartbreak. But wait — it's not actually *your* heart, right? So maybe it won't be so bad?"

For the first time in a year, her words don't hurt, not even a twinge.

I shake my head as I stand and face her. "Cole and I are friends. I ran the track because I like to run. Maybe if you found a hobby *you* liked, you could quit being so nasty."

I sit back down, grit my teeth, and stare at the screen in the front of the class with tonight's homework assignment written on it. I take my shaking hand and copy it into my notebook along with quite a few arrows that I wish I could stick into someone in the back of the room.

She's silent for the rest of class. I pack up my things early so I can bolt as soon as the bell rings. I don't want to be anywhere near Carly. I can't stand to look at her.

The hallway is crowded even though the bell just rang not even a minute ago.

"Nessa, wait!" I know it's Carly without seeing her. I've dreaded hearing that voice enough this year that I'd know it anywhere.

I should ignore her.

I should keep walking.

But I don't. I stop and turn on my heels to face the voice.

I can do this.

She runs up with a pen held out in front of her. My pen.

"Here, you dropped this at your desk."

I did? I don't remember using it. But it's definitely my pen. It's got Mom's company's name printed on the side and I use it because the ink doesn't clog up like a lot of the other pens I've used. I'm picky like that.

I take it from her.

"Thanks," I say and turn around and walk as far away from her as I can. Did I just *thank* Carly Wilkins? I wish I could go back and re-do the last minute and tell her a few not-so-nice things instead.

I look up to check the clock that hangs over the trophy case. Make sure I still have enough time to get to my locker and my next class. The numbers look solid at first, but then they start to sway back and forth. The hour and minute hands that were solid sticks become soft and bendy and my brain gets too fuzzy to figure out which way they're pointing.

My hand reaches into the bag hanging at my hip and fumbles around for the EpiPen just like it's been trained to do. Just like it did after the poisoned sandwich. My body falls slowly, at least I think it's slow until I crash to the hard floor. I cough, trying to draw in enough air to fit through my closing throat.

It's not working. The air isn't coming through.

My right hand expertly removes the safety release, swings, and jabs it into my thigh. But this time there's no click and no needle prick. My arms are getting weak, but they have enough strength to pull back and jab it into my thigh again. Still no click or prick.

It's not working.

I'm going to die.

And then Cole is standing over me. I'm losing consciousness as I feel him pull the EpiPen from my hand and hear it hit the floor. Through my closing eyes, I see him flip the safety release on another and jab it into the same thigh.

I barely hear the click and feel the prick.

But I do.

My first few breaths are slow and ragged, but I make them. Each one gets easier. Cole kneels beside me and helps me sit up against the wall of lockers. There are at least twenty kids and a few teachers around us.

"She'll need to get to the hospital," one of the teachers says, but doesn't move to help.

"I'll take her down to the office so they can call her mom," Cole says. "Can you stand?" he asks.

I nod and I try, but it's not easy. My legs feel like jelly. More than they normally do.

"Here," Cole sticks both EpiPen's in my bag, slings it over his shoulder, and wraps one of his arms around me to help me walk.

I get stronger with each step. By the time we reach the office, I feel almost normal. Well, *my* normal.

"What happened? Did you eat something?" he asks me while telling the secretary what happened and who to call.

"A pen. My pen."

"You ate a pen?" he asks.

What I touched doesn't bother me as much as the fact that the first EpiPen failed. That's how Alexis died. I should've carried a backup. How could I have been so stupid to not carry another one?

"Where did you get that other EpiPen?" I ask Cole.

He doesn't answer at first, like he's lost in his thoughts, trying to figure something out.

"She told me to follow you today..." he says, then stops.

I wait for him to finish the sentence but he doesn't and I'm too impatient to wait any longer for the answer.

"Who?"

He pauses a few more seconds, unsure.

I never get his answer. The school nurse throws the office doors open and starts an assault on every orifice I have, making sure I'm all right before Mom shows up to take me to the emergency room. Again.

* * *

After today's visit to the ER Mom tried hard to talk me out of going to Monster Monday. Almost as much as I tried to talk myself out of going.

The elephant birthday bag is light tonight. With all of the craziness going on this past week I only got two monsters finished. And only one with horns. I almost didn't come because I probably don't have enough monsters and Fiona pretty much ruined Monster Monday. Sure, there are probably kids here who didn't get her new, expensive stuffed animals, but what if they saw the ones the kids from last week got? And I show up with two cheesy hand-sewn monsters that don't even compare? I don't want them to feel like they were ripped off.

But Monster Monday is my day and I refuse to let her take that away from me. Even if no kids show up to get their monster, I'll still be there. I made a commitment and if there's one thing my dad taught me before he died, it was to honor the ones I make — even if I don't want to. If I don't have enough I can always take requests for next week.

I feel like a failure when the elevator opens and I begin the longest walk I've ever taken down the hallway of the children's wing. Ahead there's a familiar body leaning against the nurse's desk holding a purple gift bag with bright green tissue paper sticking out of it. It's almost like seeing the old me.

Twin smiles as soon as she spots me and my heart expands to fill my entire chest cavity. It pushes out the dread I feel for not having enough monsters for all of the new patients.

"Hi," I say when I reach her.

"Hi," she says back and wraps me in a hug. "I'm so sorry, Nessa."

"You don't have to be sorry. You were just looking out for me. I get that."

"I checked with the nurses. There are seven new kids this week. Did you make enough monsters?"

My smile falls from my face and I'm too slow to catch it. "I only have two. I'm hoping I can bribe a few with some extra special monsters next week. Maybe I can promise them wings or something."

"With rainbow glitter?" she asks.

I smile. That would be cool.

"Or you could always give out these monsters I made. There are six in here." She hands me the purple bag with a smile that shows all of the pride she feels.

I'm not going to lie; I cry. Not a Carly-just-made-fun-of-me-for-the-millionth-time cry. It's the best kind of cry. It's the my-best-friend-is-back-better-than-ever cry.

"Now don't get all silly mushy about it, you know what my monsters look like." Twin twists her face and sticks her tongue out of the side of her mouth. "The kids will probably throw them back at you and try to knock you out. But I do have to say, I'm definitely getting closer to professional hand-sewer level."

I step aside to let two kids by, one points a finger at Twin's bag.

"Cole told me what happened at school today," she says. "I should've been there. From now on if anyone else tries to kill my best friend, they're going to have to get through me first. I was so upset with you this weekend I figured I'd try some monster-making-hand-sewing to get over it. It helped a lot."

"I have so much to tell you," I say.

Jaz rolls her wheelie out of her room and heads our way. "Well, you'll have to wait — and tell us both because — I need to hear it, too." She smiles, but it's weak. The ends of her lips only climb half of the distance to her cheeks. They're chapped and dry.

From the amount of laughing in the common area, I'm pretty sure the kids have beat us there. Five girls and two boys today, all jumping up and down in their seats like it's Christmas morning and I'm the goofiest looking Santa Claus they've ever seen.

I pull the two monsters from the elephant bag first and hand them out, then hold the purple bag out to Twin. "You made them, you should give them out."

"Oh, no." She shakes her hands violently at me, refusing to take the bag back. "Monster Monday is all you, girl. I was just helping out. That's what friends do."

I love her to death, but Twin's monsters are a disaster. The stitching is crooked, a few are missing a leg where she cut the pattern wrong, and she tried to put horns on one that look like floppy ears instead.

The kids don't care. They don't notice the stitching and the girl who got the one with the floppy horns said she was going to call it her "monster puppy". She squeezes it under her chin and rocks it back and forth like a baby.

She sees through its flaws. Just like my friends see through mine.

Carly can say anything she wants to me. She can even cover my pen with peanut oil and try to kill me with it. It had to have been her. The pen tested positive at the hospital, and she's the only one I know of who held it before I did. I know she doesn't like me, maybe even hates me, but I never thought she'd try to kill me. What she doesn't know is that my friends and I will always be there to stop her.

25

My Eyes Find a Message

News gets old fast.

Last night Jaz told us that she was back to being a nobody and was happy about it. The reporters have stopped calling to ask for interviews and she hasn't seen her photo in the media in days.

I'm happy that she's happy, but it worries me.

A call to Cole confirmed that the traffic on our website has dropped 750,000 visitors in the last few days. He said we need a fresh story to keep people interested, like a new person dealing with a L.E.A.M. failure to feature. But where do I find one of those? Twin and Jaz have been researching Alexis's list, but they've come up empty-handed so far.

There's a lot of underwear covering Alexis's camera so it takes a few seconds of digging and a few more seconds of sweating panic to find it. I've already blocked my door with my chair so I don't have any surprise Griz visits.

The battery is dead. I shouldn't be surprised, I'm sure it hasn't been used for almost a year. There's a charger in the box that I plug in and not-so-patiently wait for the ON button to work. It takes a few minutes, but after I press it a few times the lens moves and the screen on top lights up.

Pressing the play button makes the screen on the back of the camera come to life and I'm face to face with a selfie of Alexis. Her red, curly hair is disheveled like she just woke up, but she looks beautiful with a bright white light behind her, illuminating her from behind. I never looked like this in her body. Her inner beauty shines so much, it's about to explode out of her. She holds a white piece of paper with the words "I Love You." written on it in black marker. The view screen is small, but she's close enough for me to see the tear rolling down her face. The date stamp on the camera screen says April 25th. The day she died.

I hit the button with a backward-facing arrow on it and find another selfie of Alexis. She's holding the same piece of paper, with different words written on it. 'it's OK.' The tear is gone.

In the photo before that, her sign says 'Whatever happens,'.

I've been flipping through them backward.

Whatever happens, it's OK. I love you.

She knew she was in danger. And this was her message. A tear rolls down her cheek again, only this time I'm the one making it. I wonder if her dad even looked at the pictures on here before he wrapped the camera in its perfect wrapping paper and bow. Maybe he couldn't do it.

I hit the backward arrow again to see if there's any more of the message but the picture before that one is of an X. It looks like a close-up photo of a street sign. I hit the button again to find a picture of Meg at a coffee shop and the one before that has Toby standing against a locker in a school I don't recognize.

The photo of the X bothers me. It doesn't fit in with any other photo I've seen that Alexis has taken. They all have people. They all tell a story.

218

Maybe the photo of the X is its own story.

I use the forward arrow and return to the picture to study it closely. Its date stamped April 24. The day Seymour Rice died.

I squint to see it closer. The letter is white and the background of the sign is green. The letter is at the end of the word, so all that's visible is the X on the left, the edge of the sign, and what looks like a field and some trees in the background.

What if X marks the spot and Alexis is showing where she hid Seymour's drive?

There's a share button on the back of the camera so I email it to myself. I'll get it printed. Poster-sized if I need to. I've got to see the background clearer. There has to be some clue that will help me figure out where that sign is.

I also forward it to Mr. O'Riley's private cell phone and ask if he's ever seen the sign before.

Now all I can do is wait. Wait for the photo to be printed, wait for Mr. O'Riley to reply.

I do what I usually do to pass the time.

I make more monsters.

* * *

219

Carly was absent from school yesterday. I heard a few whispers behind me in French class that she got suspended. I have no idea for how long or why, but Mrs. Beatty doesn't say her name during attendance in French class this morning. Like she's just gone from existence.

I don't know what I'll say to her when I finally see her.

"Hey. I know you tried to kill me." That doesn't show how mad and upset I am. If she would put peanut oil on my pen what would stop her from putting it on my chair? Or my locker handle? And now it makes me wonder if she was the one who put it on my sandwich the first time I had an allergy attack. We have the same lunch period.

Twin says I should tell the police. And if not them, then at least the principal. She should be expelled. But I have no proof. I have the pen and the toxicology report from the ER, but I can't prove Carly is the person who handed it to me. I told my mom I picked the pen up from the floor. She'd never let me leave my room again if she knew someone gave it to me on purpose.

It's not that I think Carly should get away with anything.

I'm just not sure how to deal with it yet. Her being suspended gives me a little more time to figure it out.

Cole drops his lunch tray to the table and slides into the bench across from me.

"Have you heard back from Mr. O'Riley about that X yet?"

"He didn't recognize it." I try to hide my disappointment but I don't think it's working.

"Think Toby would drive us out to look for it in his car? Did you hear it growl every time he hit the gas? I'm still dreaming about it," Cole gushes. I roll my eyes and don't care if he sees.

"I'm not asking Toby for any more favors. He's done enough for us. You do realize this is way more important than cool cars, right?"

"Is it?" Cole asks. "When was the picture taken?"

"April 24. Same day Seymour Rice died in that accident."

"Do you think Alexis would've hidden the disk right where she got it from him? And maybe took that picture to tell someone where it was?" Cole asks as he shoves a spoonful of corn into his mouth. The last few words come out in a garbled mess but I figure it out.

"That's what I'm thinking. But why wouldn't she take a picture of the whole sign if she wanted to show us where it is?" I ask.

"Maybe she couldn't. Maybe she was afraid of making it too obvious or hid it there until she could think of a better place, but ran out of time before she could."

"Maybe. Probably. I don't know. She should've come straight home and posted it all on her website right away!" The cafeteria gets silent and I realize too late that I yelled the last few words. I'm standing, face flushed and red with rage.

"But she didn't," Cole says quietly. His calm tone is the complete opposite of my outburst and makes me feel even more like an out-of-control idiot standing here in the middle of 400 staring eyes.

I sit back down beside him and don't verbalize the words going through my brain. The words scare me. They're probably the reason why I'm so angry, with sweat pouring from everywhere right now.

Not because *she* didn't get Seymour's files posted before she died.

I didn't.

26

My Brain Gets Blown to Bits

Mom's not home when I walk through the front door.

Perfect.

I haven't been down in our musty basement for years, and I've never been a fan of the place, but I'm sure that this is where Mom hid the picture frames I had her get rid of after the accident.

I figure I've got a good two hours before she gets home to dig them back out, dust them off, and put them back on the shelves and the tables. Then hopefully our house will look like the home it used to be.

Our house is old and the basement has never been finished. Just a concrete slab on the floor and bare wood beams on the ceiling and walls. A single light bulb hangs down from the middle of the ceiling, casting a creepy shadow on the boxes and furniture. Mom moved almost all of Dad's things down here after the accident.

When I see things that were his, it hurts. Physically, mentally, and just an all-over hurt. I spent all day at school preparing myself for this, but now that I'm down here staring down his favorite recliner, I realize you can't prepare for something like this. I run my fingers over the worn fuzziness where his arm would rest every night after dinner.

There are boxes piled high all around. I have no idea where to start looking. Mom's not the most organized person; nothing's labeled.

The first box I open has his old magazines. Magazines about Astronomy, old cars, and a few about motorcycles. Stuff that I have no interest in. They're over a year old; I'm pretty sure *no one* would have any interest in them. Mom should've just thrown them out and saved me from having to look through them.

After I move that box from the pile it shows the tops of two more below it and miraculously, one is labeled pictures.

This is it!

One by one, I pull photos out and remember how he showed me how to catch the giant fish I'm holding in the first one. And the vacation we took to the ocean the summer before he died.

But seeing pictures of him wasn't my fear. And it turns out; I had no reason to be scared. The photos of me in the old Nessa body don't pierce my heart or send me into a full-on panic attack like I thought they would.

They don't bother me at all.

But I remember there being more picture frames than there are in this box. I still haven't found Mom and Dad's wedding photos, or the one of him when he graduated college. I open the box next to it and hope it has the rest. The sooner I get out of this basement, the happier I'll be.

The next box is just a pile of papers. I don't even bother to dig to the bottom to see if there are any pictures underneath. I'm ready to get out of here. One box is going to have to be enough for now. I close the first flap and a word catches my attention before I close the second.

No way.

Dr. Hursh has been telling Mom for months that my brain isn't fragile any more, but I don't believe him now.

Because this small piece of paper has just blown my poor, fragile brain to bits.

27

My Mouth Confesses

Mom opens the front door and stops suddenly, staring at me staring at her from where I sit crying on the couch.

"What is it? What's wrong Vanessa?"

"Why didn't you tell me Dad had lupus?" I hold up the prescription paperwork for L.E.A.M. as her bag falls from her hand and hits the hardwood floor with a thud.

"You know he had such a hard time talking about stuff like that. And he was worried that it would put too much stress on you. He made me swear not to tell. He said he'd tell you when the time was right. But then it was too late." She pauses and closely examines a fingernail. "He was gone and I figured it didn't matter anymore. And then

227

you didn't want to talk about him — would knowing have made anything different?" Mom asks, sitting next to me, embracing me in a side hug.

"Then, no. Now, yes."

"Why?"

I never thought I would tell Mom any of this, because — well, she *is* the Griz. But maybe she's what I need right now. A little momma grizzly bear action to help me find Seymour's files because I'm not doing so well at finding them on my own.

I tell her everything.

She doesn't ask me why I didn't tell her any of this before tonight. I think we're both guilty of that. There's that saying that two wrongs make a right. Or maybe it's that they don't. Whatever it is, I feel like we have an understanding. I forgive her and she forgives me. We seal the deal with a hug that feels way overdue.

"Do you think they killed your father?" she asks.

I was so blown away by the fact that he had lupus and had taken L.E.A.M. before the accident that my brain never thought that far into it.

But now...

What if they did?

"I don't know," I answer.

"So where do we start?" Mom asks.

"Hang on a sec." I run to my room and get the poster-sized print of the X that Twin and I picked up at the drug store on our way home from school.

Mom takes it out to the kitchen and unrolls it, laying it out flat on the table. I watch her in silence, hoping for something positive. Can I get a gasp? Or an excited jump?

"Nessa!" she finally exclaims. Her hands slap together in excitement. "I think I know where this is! See this little bit of red back here behind these trees? It looks like a big red barn I used to pass when I'd have to drive to the Indy office on Route 70." I squint my eyes and look closer. I don't recognize it – I hardly ever go on Route 70, but her being excited about it is getting me excited.

"I bet that's it!" We took Route 70 to Muncie when Toby drove us there a few days ago. It would make sense. Maybe that's where Alexis met Seymour. "We have to go!"

"Look outside, it's almost dark. I know this stretch of road and it's poorly lit. We'll have to wait until tomorrow. I'll pick you up from school and we'll drive straight there."

Mom and I spend the next hour finding the rest of the picture frames in the basement, cleaning them off, crying, and putting them back up around the house. She doesn't ask what changed my mind about them and I don't tell her.

I'm not sure I know the whole answer.

I'm halfway up the stairs to bed when Mom calls to me.

"Wait, Nessa, I forgot a letter came for you today."

The envelope has no return address, the only clue I could find was that it was mailed from Columbus yesterday.

The card inside had the same handwriting as the note Fiona left for me at the hospital. I remember it clearly. My body breaks out in goosebumps when it occurs to me that Fiona knows where I live. I'm not safe here. I drop the envelope and the card as soon as I pull it out, like it's on fire and burnt my fingers.

There are only three words written on it.

Time is up.

* * *

Sleep won me over quickly tonight. Massive amounts of crying can wear a person out. I must not be too deep into sleep when my cell phone rings because it yanks me back out. At first, I'm confused and think it's my alarm, but after about the third ring I figure it out and answer.

"Hello?" I didn't even think to look at the caller ID on the front before I answered. I hate trying to figure out who I'm talking to. I quickly pull it away from my face and see Mr. O'Riley's name.

Does he realize it's almost midnight on a school night?

"Hello, Vanessa. I'm sorry for calling so late."

I mumble words even I don't understand.

This better be good.

"I just wanted to give you a quick update that I snuck into Fiona's office when she went out for lunch today and stole some paperwork. There's a lot of files and it's taking a while to go through them. Toby's here helping. I'll let you know if we find anything useful. Just — don't lose hope."

I hear the connection die before I have a chance to mumble anything else.

The only hope I've lost now is that I'll get any sleep tonight.

Thanks to that phone call getting my brain to rest is going to be impossible.

* * *

"What are you doing?" I ask Twin. I didn't find anything weird about her holding the front door open for me to walk through this morning. I didn't even think there was anything odd about her punching my locker combination into the keypad so it pops open for her. She's always known my code. But now she's pulling my books out from the top shelf and stops to think.

"Do you have English second period?"

"What are you doing?" I ask louder and reach around her to grab my English book.

"No!" Twin slaps my arm!

I coil back, livid. "MADDELYN ROSE SANDERS! Stop acting like an idiot and give me my English book!"

She stares back at me, as still as a statue, but doesn't give me the book.

And then I know why.

"The Griz. She put you up to this, didn't she?"

"She called my mom this morning. Said she was worried about you touching anything at school. I've got three spare EpiPen's in my bag just in case." She shoves one in the messenger bag hanging at my side.

"Let me guess," I say. "she's making you follow me to all of my classes and open all of the doors for me. Wow. And what does she expect me to do once I'm in there? Stand for the entire class so my body doesn't touch a chair?"

"Oh, no. You can sit. Cole went in early and scrubbed down the seat and desk with sanitizer."

I scream. Loud.

So not only is the Griz an over-protective maniac, she's turning my friends into them too? I get it, I really do. She's my mother and my life is in danger. Protecting me is what she's supposed to do. I'd be upset if she didn't. But Twin and Cole?

Twin looks at me, then shoves the two books she took from my locker into my arms. "She cares about you, Nessa. We all do. We want you to stick around for a while. Think about what it was like to lose your dad. Would you wish losing someone like that on anyone else? Especially us?"

I shake my head. Even a year later the pain of his loss is still there, every time I see his name, smell his favorite cologne, or see one of the eight million things on this Earth that reminds me of him.

"Then let us help keep you alive."

And Twin always said I was the smart one.

* * *

"So your mom is picking us up after school to check out the sign?" Cole asks as he crunches down on a large carrot from his lunch tray.

"Not us, *me*. She's picking *me* up after school to check out the sign."

"Will you stop trying to leave me out of everything?" Cole stops chewing and stares me down. "I sanitized four desks for you today already. FOUR! Not to mention how many records I hacked into, and what about Friday when I skipped school to help you out? I'm as much involved in this as you. You think you can do this yourself, but why should you have to? Alexis tried to do it by herself and see how far that got her? You, me, Twin, and Jaz. We're all in this now. Together."

I'm not sure why I don't trust my friends to make their own choices. If they didn't want to help then they wouldn't be here right now. They want to help. Let them.

His brown eyes wait patiently.

I drop my gaze to the table. "I'm sorry. Yes, you can go with us if that's what you really want to do. Thanks for wiping the desks. So if my Mom gave Twin three EpiPens, how many did she load you up with?"

I'm sure he answers because I see his lips move, but I don't hear it. I'm lost in an incomplete thought.

"Wait," I interrupt. "The other day. When you saved me with that EpiPen, you didn't tell me where you got it."

"She made me swear not to tell you," he says. All eating at this table has stopped. Pretty sure we're not getting the nutrients we need today.

"Whoever gave you that EpiPen and told you to follow me around knew that Carly put peanut oil on that pen. Maybe they know more. Maybe they're on our side and can help us. You have to tell me, Cole."

"Fine. I'll tell you." But he pauses like he's still trying to justify it in his head.

"The bell is going to ring in like one minute. Spit it out."

"Carly. Carly gave me the EpiPen, showed me how to use it, and told me to follow you around that day."

28

My Ears Hear the Bad and the Good

The Carly thing gives me plenty to think about on our drive to where Mom thinks the 'X' sign is. But the more I think about it, the less it makes sense. Why would she give me the pen with the peanut oil and then give Cole everything he needed to save me from it? Why hand me the pen in the first place? Did she know my own EpiPen would malfunction before it did?

"You're quiet," Twin says to me in Mom's backseat.

We've been in the car for over a half-hour and are traveling down Route 70. Mom and Cole have been chatting in the front seats, but I haven't listened to a word they've said. I'm too absorbed.

Keeping my voice low so Mom doesn't hear, I tell Twin about how Cole went straight to the principal after Mom rushed me to the ER. When Cole told him what Carly did they suspended her from school for a week and they switched her schedule around so we wouldn't have any more classes together. Or lunch. My life is now Carly Wilkins free.

"But why would she do that?" Twin asks.

"If I knew, I wouldn't be this quiet," I answer. "I've been trying to figure it out."

"It's up here," Mom says from the driver's seat. "I'll pull over when we get to it. I always thought it was weird because usually speed limit signs say 'Speed Limit' and then the number. But this one says 'Speed Max' and the number. I'm sure that's where the 'X' on the sign is from."

"Remember what Mrs. Rice said," I say. "It's a black drive; looks like a black stick. With blue stripes down the side."

"A black stick? It'll be a needle in a haystack in that grass," Cole says, pointing ahead at the white sign that says 'Speed Max'. He's right. The grass surrounding the sign is higher than my knees.

Mom slows the car down and pulls it over to the side of the highway.

"Get on your hands and knees," I instruct as soon as we're all out of the car and surrounding the metal sign pole.

"Are you sure she would hide it *here*?" Twin asks. "There's no way we'll find something so small in this high grass."

"I'm not sure of anything." I run back to the car to get Alexis's camera. I've been keeping it in my bag lately. I don't know why. It's not like I've taken any pictures with it. I hold my eye to the viewfinder, using it to recreate Alexis's photo and match the picture. "This is definitely where she took the photo. Does anyone have a better place to look?"

They shake their heads.

"Then on your hands and knees." I dive to the ground first, checking around the base of the metal pole. My fingers poke around the dirt, pressing and feeling to see if any of it seems different in any way. But mother Earth on Route 70 seems untouched by human hands. I even try to dig some out with my fingers but find no black stick with blue stripes.

The four of us work silently for a little over a half-hour when Twin suggests we give up.

"Nessa, this is impossible. Even if it is here, we'll never find that tiny drive."

"But what about Jaz? If we don't find those files, she'll keep getting sicker."

"Honey, you don't know that." Mom sits in the middle of the tall grass with her legs bent in front of her. The grass is so high, all that shows of her is her shoulders and head. Her hair blows in the breeze left by cars driving past. "Even if we do find the files, Dr. Rice's research is just that. It's still research. A company would still need to manufacture the cure he came up with, do trials, get government approvals, and that takes time."

I stand and start searching the pole and the back of the sign, thinking that maybe the drive is taped to it somehow.

"It's kismet, Mom. There was a reason that I got Alexis's body and that reason was so I could save Jaz and the millions of other people that this drug is destroying."

"I don't think you're going to find your reason on Route 70," Cole says as he stands and puts his hands up in a surrendering gesture. "It may have been here a year ago when Alexis put it here, but it's not anymore."

The three of them return to the car and give me time to come to peace with the fact that I'll never find Seymour

Rice's research. Failure is a hard pill to swallow. I'm grateful that I can't hear what people driving by at 'Speed Max 65' are saying when they pass the girl standing at the sign, crying enough tears to flood the highway.

There's that girl who can't possibly live up to the amazing girl whose body she took. The one who gave her sick friend hope and now has to tell her she was wrong. You know, that girl who traded in a broken body for a broken heart.

* * *

My cell phone finally lights up with Mr. O'Riley's name on Friday night. I can't pick it up fast enough.

He's the only hope I have left.

"I finally located some information about Seymour Rice, but it's not much." He doesn't bother with formalities, just jumps right into the meat of things. "I found a memo to Fiona from one of her employees dated April 25 saying the Rice research hasn't been located and that they've exhausted all of their efforts. I'm sorry I'm not calling with better news."

"So it proves and tells us nothing," I whisper. I'd meant to say it louder, but my chest is constricted and the sound won't come out. The pain I feel there makes me wonder if my heart's cracking in half; one half for Jaz, the other for Alexis.

"Just that they were trying to find his research. They don't even say his full name, so nothing that would hold up in court," Mr. O'Riley says.

I thank Mr. O'Riley for the information and for the camera, then I burrow my head in the pillows on my bed and cry myself to sleep. I don't bother to look up at the stars on my ceiling. Even they won't comfort me tonight.

* * *

My phone buzzing and vibrating next to my head wakes me up.

At first, I think I'm late for school, but then I realize it's Saturday. I hate waking up early on Saturday.

The sun is barely up. It's just starting to creep its way in through my curtains. Who would even be awake this early to call? Whoever it is, they're not on my good list.

My arm windmills over to the table and slams down on the phone, pulling it to my face. I have to squint to read it. My eyes haven't fully adjusted to being awake yet; they're not ready for the bright screen.

241

It's a text from Jaz.

I have important news. Can you visit today?

Mom left for a few hours this morning. Something for work. I'm sure she's gone already, which leaves me no way to get there. That, and the Griz made me swear for an hour yesterday that I would absolutely not leave the house or open the door while she was gone. For anyone, even Twin. She said she was arming the house alarm. She's got it set up so she gets a message on her phone anytime it's disarmed. I'm a prisoner here.

But we all know I'm smarter than that, right?

I hate to wake so many people up early on a Saturday morning, but I need to get out of this house.

By 9:30 a.m. Cole has figured out how to disarm my house without alerting my mom. At 9:45 a.m. I hop into the passenger seat of Toby's car that growls. I'm sure the last thing a sixteen-year-old guy wants to do on a Saturday afternoon is hang out in a hospital lobby, but he's the first yes I got. Cole's parents were busy and if I asked McKenna she would tell the Griz I was planning to leave. I plan to make it a super-short hospital visit so I don't get grounded for life.

And I dread it.

I've already made up my mind that I'm going to tell Jaz I've failed her. I don't want her hoping we'll find something when won't.

The walk from the elevator to Jaz's room is the worst seventy-three steps I've ever taken. Each time my left foot hits the floor, I try to convince myself not to mention it to her. But when my right foot hits the floor after it, I tell myself I have to. It's kind of like an eenie-meenie-miney-mo thing. Which ever foot makes my last step is the one I'm going to listen to.

Turns out I end with both feet hitting the ground at the same time when I stop short inside of her room. It's been five days since I've seen her, but she looks like it's been five hundred. There are more machines hooked up to her today, not just her wheelie and the oxygen. Her face looks sunken in like her insides have taken a vacation and left without her skin.

"Nessa. Thank you — for coming. I have — good news — and bad. Mom? Would you give — us a minute?" I give her an air kiss and pull the chair beside her bed right up to it as her Mom leaves the room. "Which — do you — want to hear — first?"

"Give me the bad first," I say. Lately, bad news is my specialty. I've got to be used to it by now. One more sad thing is just going to make my ever-growing list a little longer. I want to get it over with. Like ripping off a band-aid as fast as you can so it doesn't hurt as much.

"Good choice. Today's — my last day here," she says.

"How is that bad news? You get to go home!" I squeal.

"It's not — like that. We're moving — to Pennsylvania."

"What? Why?"

"My mom — thinks she found — a better doctor — for me there." She doesn't finish. The tears rolling down her cheeks finish the sentence for her.

"Jaz! You can't move so far away!" I jump out of my seat, knocking my bag to the floor. It clunks when it hits, probably Alexis's camera. I don't even care. I never use it anyway.

"I'm tired — of living like this. And they say — the chemo's not working. They have an — experimental treatment — they're going to try."

"I'll call Dr. Hursh! See if he can find you a new body, too. I'll even give you mine if he thinks it would work."

"And give up my chance to be this amazing strong black woman? I don't want — yours. Look at — what you've — done to it. It's hideous." Jaz laughs a soundless, hollow laugh that makes her start coughing. I sit and try to calm down while I wait for her to get her breath back. "Don't you — want to — hear my — good news?" she asks when she finally gets enough air for the words to come out.

I nod because I know I won't be able to talk without falling apart.

"I found — my lion tamer."

"You — what? Who?"

"Remember — that boy who — would always — push his — sister to Monster — Monday? The tall — one?"

"Mya's brother? The guy who never talks?" I ask.

"Well, he — does talk. His name — is Luis. And he's super-hot — super-sweet — and turns out — super-in — love with me." Jaz smiles again and this time it's a different smile than I've ever seen on her. Looks like she's super-in love right back. "We're going — to try a long -distance — relationship."

"That's amazing, Jaz! I'm just — kind of in shock right now. How did it happen?"

"He showed up — one afternoon — and we started — talking. Isn't it — funny — how something — can be —

right in front — of us the — whole time and — we never — see it until — we really — look?"

"Jaz!" I jump up from the chair. The back of my legs hit it and send it flying across the room with a giant screech. I reach down for my bag and dig out the camera. I flip the switch to 'on', and the screen lights up. It says there are 40 pictures taken on the memory card and only 64 more available to take. I press the power button on the camera again to turn it back off and pull the memory card out.

The card says it has 128 GB of space on it. There should be room for thousands of photos on here, not just a little over a hundred like the camera says. Other files are filling up this card!

X marks the spot.

And I was looking in the wrong one.

I give Jaz the fastest air kiss I've ever attempted as I shove the card back into the camera and put it into my bag.

"Promise me you'll stay here until you hear from me? If you can't do it for me, then do it for Luis the lion tamer."

She smiles bigger than her face. Brighter than the sun. Stronger than lupus.

"I'll stick — around as long — as I can."

29

My Feet Fly

"Buckle up." Toby already has his fastened and is out of the parking lot before my phone finishes dialing Cole's number.

I barely give him time to answer it. "I have Seymour's research files. Alexis hid them on her camera's memory card. Can you get them off and uploaded to the website as soon as possible? And write up some press releases while we're on our way so they're ready to go out as soon as the files are there? Make sure you mention that the information is free. And make sure you mention that it's a safe and natural alternative to L.E.A.M. and that it was discovered and developed by Seymour Rice, who lost his life to make this information available."

"I got it. Just make sure Toby drives carefully. Don't want him messing up my dream car."

"Ugh! Just get writing ready!" I yell.

Cole gives me his address and I repeat it to Toby. "Get onto 270, take the Little Turtle Way exit, then make a left at the first light."

I take my bag from the floor by my feet and lay it in my lap. I don't want to step on the camera by accident. It's too important.

We're off the exit in minutes and only a few streets away from Cole's house when I see the dashboard.

1:34.

My fear of the numbers distracts me from seeing the white car miss the stop sign we pass.

"Duck!" Toby yells and presses his foot down hard. His car growls in response and speeds up faster than I can think. The white car coming at us hits the back end of the passenger side instead of my door. It throws Toby's car into a fast spin and before I have my head lowered into my lap, the back end of Toby's side of the car slams into a telephone pole and stops.

"Are you okay?" he asks. He looks dazed, but not hurt. I nod. I'm a little dizzy from the spinning, but other than that I feel all right. "Are we close enough that we can run the rest of the way? If they're not hurt they'll have us cornered soon."

"Thank you for saving me, Toby."

"I took a defensive driving course after I heard what happened to you in that first accident. I wasn't about to let them kill Alexis again. Or you. They're climbing out of the car. You'd better get going."

I lean over and give him a quick air kiss, strap the long handle of my messenger bag over my shoulder and across my chest so they can't grab it and take off. Two men approach me from across the street where the white car ended up. The back door opens. I don't wait long enough to see who gets out, but I can't miss the feet below the door covered in leopard print.

So sorry, Fiona Gray. Not today.

One of the men reaches behind him like he's going to pull out a gun. He wouldn't dare. Would he? There are at least ten people in various places, all looking at the car accident. If he has one, I take off running before he has a chance to use it.

I underestimate the men. They're fast. But believe it or not, I'm faster. I can cut through the two houses up ahead and run through the back yards to get to Cole's house quicker.

I'm pretty sure I'm breaking the land-speed record. I run faster than I've ever run in my life. Faster than I've ever run in my old Nessa body. I run fast for Jaz. For Alexis and Seymour. For Mr. O'Riley, Mary Rice, Toby, and even Meg. And for all of the other lives the files in this camera will change forever.

It slows me down a little, but I pull my phone out while I run and call Cole to tell him I'm coming through the back door. I want him to have it open for me since I have some unwanted company.

Not only does he have the back door open for me, but he's got his phone out, ready to arm the house alarm as soon as I get in. I fly inside the house as he slams the sliding glass door closed behind me and dig the camera out of the bag slung across my stomach.

Cole's ready. He's got his laptop set up on the kitchen counter and has the camera's memory card inserted before the guys chasing me begin shooting bullets through the glass door I just came through. The glass shatters into a million pieces at my feet. I've never been so terrified in my life. For a moment, I stare at the bullet hole in the kitchen wall before I think to duck behind the counter.

I'm pretty sure *this* is the time I'm going to die. I've had so many close calls before, but for real. This is going to be it.

Cole sits beside me on the floor behind the counter with his laptop in his lap. He whispers, "The files were there. Now they're out in the world. You did it, Nessa. I'm uploading the press releases now."

He says more, but his words are replaced by the sound of sirens. I let myself hope that soon I may walk back out from behind this counter. I close my eyes and think about Alexis's last photos and the words she held in her hand.

She's right.

It's okay now.

With my old body, with this body, or with no body. It doesn't matter anymore.

Everything's okay.

30

My Arms Hug the Horrible

"You're bleeding," Cole says.

I am?

My forehead stings. I didn't notice it with glass shattering and thinking I was going to die.

There's noise, lots of it. People talking, yelling at us. They ask if there's anyone else in here and if we're okay. Cole answers their questions while he soaks a towel in the sink for my head. Suddenly we're surrounded by policemen, Cole's parents who were upstairs when they heard their glass door shatter, and Toby who ran after me. Just not nearly as fast.

A policewoman with long, straight red hair pulled into a tight ponytail kneels to where I cower behind the counter. She takes the wet towel from my shaking hand and presses it to my head, applying more pressure. Even now that I know it's over, my limbs shake uncontrollably.

But it's not over.

Cole bends down to pick up his laptop so I try to get his attention without the policewoman noticing. It's not easy. I finally grab the pant leg of his jeans and yank them as hard as I can.

"We have to go," I say to him when he looks over. The woman holding the towel to my head doesn't see or hear. She's leaning the other way, telling someone else an ambulance is on the way.

Hopefully not for me. I won't be around by the time they get here.

"Could your dad drive us somewhere?" I whisper to Cole.

"Now? For what? They aren't going to let us leave!" Cole whispers. The policewoman has her full attention back on me. I hope he doesn't think he's going to get an answer now.

"I'm thinking we should get you to the couch until the EMTs arrive to check you out," she says and I nod. The

253

movement makes me woozy, but I can't tell her that. There's no time as it is. Once Fiona realizes that her reputation is crumbling around her, she'll be out for blood. And for once it won't be mine.

The officer helps move me to the other room, onto the couch. On my way out of the kitchen, I see Cole talking to his dad. Toby catches my eye from across the room where he's leaning, holding up a wall. A smile covers his face. He's not upset that his expensive car is mangled around a telephone pole, I'm sure he's glad he could help because he loved Alexis and this was her cause.

I'm lying on the couch with the now bloody towel still on my head when I wonder if they realize they need to sneak me out of here. Officer Wendling, or super-police-woman, hasn't left my side. She's like a ninja. Always watching. Never leaving. Ready to take out anyone who looks at me funny. Where was she weeks ago when I could have used her?

I can't see Cole or his dad. It's hard to see anything lying on a couch.

"I have to use the bathroom," I tell her and attempt to sit up.

"I don't know if that's such a good idea. I hear sirens in the distance, they'll be here in just a minute or two to get you all checked out."

That's what I'm afraid of. Once they get here, I'll never escape.

"Not soon enough. The Mariano's will never forgive me if I pee all over their couch."

She nods. "Can I help you get there?"

"Um — no thanks. I'm fine, really. I need to find Cole so he can show me where the bathroom is."

"I think that's his mom over there, I bet she can tell us." She stands up and walks across the room to her.

I need Cole.

I'll never be able to end this thing for good without him. We put Seymour's research online and hopefully, soon the whole world will see it and begin to manufacture a lupus drug that will actually work. It might make Fiona lose her job, but it doesn't hold her accountable for what she did to Seymour and Alexis. Or what she's been trying to do to me.

I finally see Cole. He's on the opposite side of the large living room and points to a door behind the counter we hid behind only minutes ago. My first few steps to him are wobbly, and my jelly legs almost throw me to the

255

ground on the fourth step but someone catches me from behind.

Toby.

"Can you follow me to the garage?" I ask him quietly.

"Only if you stop walking like a newborn deer." He sets me upright and holds the top of my arms to steady me. "Are you good now?"

"I'm alright." And I mean it this time. Out of the corner of my eye, I see an EMT coming through the same door, trying to fit a stretcher through it. Super-police-woman heads straight for them.

Cole catches up to us when I'm about five steps away from the door. "Don't leave your laptop here, just in case," I tell Cole. There are too many important files on it to just leave it lying on the kitchen counter.

He scoops it up on the way by and I grab my bag that now lies on the floor. I'm not leaving Alexis's camera either.

The more steps I take the stronger I feel. The door in the kitchen opens to the garage where Cole's dad waits for us to get into his running car.

As Mr. Mariano pulls out onto the street there are at least five police cars and an ambulance with their lights dancing, and even more policemen. A few of them push the men that shot at me into the back of two squad cars. I'm relieved that they were caught, but I don't see the leopard print shoes anywhere. Or the fake doctor that wore them.

"Am I going to get in trouble for letting you leave?" Mr. Mariano leans over and asks me from the front seat.

"I hope not."

"Where to?"

"4352 Sequoia Drive," I say. "It's not far."

* * *

I rode my bike to this house hundreds of times. I remember the address like it's tattooed on my wrist.

The winding driveway is lined with trees so thick you can barely see past the trunks. I always loved this house for those trees. They cover almost every inch of the yard except where the house sits.

"Follow me to the back door, they won't answer if we use the front."

There's a little path of flat stones leading us to the back door of the house.

Mark answers when I knock.

"Hey, Nessa. She's in her room." He looks oddly at the strange group standing on his back porch.

I go first because I know where her bedroom is. Cole's behind me, followed by Toby, then Mr. Mariano. I wave to her grandmother in the living room we pass by on our way through. She looks away from the TV and lifts her hand for a half-wave. Her eyebrow takes a nosedive as she tries to figure out why four people are walking through her house.

I don't knock on her door. Her attempt to kill me took away all of the formalities between us.

"What took you so long?" Carly says, looking up from a book. She pulls her air pods out and lays them on the bed beside her. "What's up with the man slash boy squad? Are these your bodyguards or something?"

"Why did you try to kill me then save my life a minute later?" I'm not here to make nice. I just want to know what she knows. Carly and I may not be friends anymore, but I still know who she is. And she's not the kind of person who would kill anyone. Even me.

"Nessa!"

A voice from behind Mr. Mariano stops me from saying more. Twin! She pushes through the boys and hugs me, then glares at Carly.

"I came to ask her why she tried to kill you."

"So I take it I'm not going to get any Christmas cards from either of you?"

"Fiona Gray got away," I tell Carly. "I figured if she's mad enough, she might come after you because you didn't finish the job."

"Well, I haven't seen her." Carly stands up from where she was sitting on her bed and opens a little drawer on her nightstand. She digs around for a minute, then throws a small memory card at Cole. She had to know he couldn't catch it, his laptop is under his arm. Toby reaches in front of him and makes the catch.

"There's your proof. Fiona hired me to kill you at school. She said she needed someone 'inside' who knew what you did, and where you went day in and day out. She offered to pay me a lot of money to do it and told me she'd buy me a plane ticket to go see my Mom. At first, I thought I could do it. But then I realized that I like you more than I like my mother. And way more than I like that fake Fiona chick."

She pauses and purses her lips together.

"And who could I make fun of at school if you were dead?"

I had to laugh at that, even though this situation is anything but funny.

"So I figured I'd help you instead. Mark rigged a tiny camera to my necklace. I recorded her telling me how to spread the peanut oil on the pen, how much to use, and how to fix your Epi-Pen so it wouldn't work. I knew she'd follow up, maybe even have spies there to make sure I did it, so I had to convince her that I really did try, and Cole just happened to step in at the right time and save you. That card has the video. She admits she was trying to have you killed. So that's it. Put it online. Fry her butt. Attempted murder should get her at least ten years."

Ten years would give us time to look for more proof in Alexis's murder. And Seymour Rice's.

"Why did you wait almost a week to give us this?" Cole says with traces of anger in his voice.

"I was waiting for an apology. From both of you." She looks at me, then Twin. "Thought maybe I could trade it for the video."

She almost killed me. And she wants *me* to apologize to *her*? For what? But then it comes to me, like a brick hitting me on the forehead. For the lunch table.

I take a deep breath and apologize for switching lunch tables and not asking her to join us. How many years ago? I don't even remember. Twin looks at me weirdly but adds her apology to mine. It's kind of amazing how long someone can hold a grudge.

I don't want to cry in front of Carly, that would admit weakness and I know she'll *never* let me forget it, but I do it anyway. I even hug her. She stands as stiff as a 2x4 but relaxes a little before I let go. I think I even get a quarter of a hug back.

I turn to give Twin a chance at a Carly hug because I know how much Carly will hate it.

"Uploaded and published," Cole says, holding his open laptop in his palm.

I just hope they catch her — she's probably halfway to Mexico by now.

All thanks to a girl named Alexis and her body that I happen to inhabit.

31

My Heart Has Hope

Everyone else leaves out of the back door, but I hang back. I tell them I'll meet them in the car in a minute. Carly and I need to talk. Even though I'm sure, besides hugging me, it's the last thing on earth she wants to do.

I sit on the edge of her bed and grab her air pods from her. She was reaching for them, and I don't want her to use them to block me out.

"We have nothing to talk about," she says sharply. "Can I have my pods back?" Her hand is held out to me, waiting for them.

"I am sorry, like more than you know. I should've seen you needed a friend more than ever instead of just abandoning you. I hope you can forgive me."

"Me saving your life was me saying I forgive you," she says.

"Yeah, but you were the one who tried to kill me."

She smiles. Not the I-just-made-fun-of-you-for-the-millionth-time smile that I've seen so much lately, but a genuine Carly smile. The one I used to see when I'd ride my bike here on a Saturday afternoon so we could play Monopoly for hours on her back porch. Or go off into her woods to look for anything living and breathing that we could make into a pet.

"How would I save your life if you weren't in danger of dying first?"

I roll my eyes.

"Wanna hang out sometime?" I ask.

"Maybe." But she smiles that good smile again. And as I walk back through the house to get to the back door I have hope. Hope that maybe we will.

My steps on the flat stone path seem lighter on the way back out.

Maybe because I almost feel like Carly and I can put the past behind us and be somewhat friends again. Or maybe because for the first time in a year, Jaz has hope. Or that with Fiona's deeds plastered all over the internet, all of the money and fame she killed to get mean nothing. She can't use any of it in a prison cell.

Fingernails dig into my arm and pull me back into the woods from behind.

I stumble, and as I look down leopard print fills my brain with black clouds of dread.

Fiona.

Her grip is strong and after all I've put my body through today, the energy isn't there to fight back.

"No one can see me kill you here."

Her fingernails scrape both of my arms as she throws my body up against a nearby tree trunk. All of her body weight holds me there. The back of my head throbs where it hit and got scraped by the jagged bark.

"Give me his research. I know you have it," Fiona growls.

"I don't..." I struggle through the pain to say. I'm feeling dizzy but fight against it. Wait. She doesn't know it's already online?

"You're lying again." Her eyes meet mine and they lock. I pretend that we're having a staring contest because if

I'm going to lose my life right now at least I can say I won something first.

And I win. She blinks first.

"I have it, and I'll give it to you if you let me go," I say. She releases her grip. "This was Alexis's fight, not mine. I just want everyone to leave me alone." I don't know if this will work but it's the only chance I have. I throw my hand into my bag, scrambling around frantically searching. It finds the pen and expertly flips the lid without me having to look at it first.

She takes a step back to give me room but doesn't release my other wrist. I follow her by stepping away from the tree.

I pull the pen out, hoping it's fast enough for her to think I have a computer drive then throw my arm, stabbing it into her side. She cries out and her body stiffens as I hold it there, hoping to inject her with enough of the epinephrine to scare her. It works. Her eyes show every bit of panic I hoped they would. But both of us know this won't stop her for long.

I use the last of my energy and one of Alexis's self-defense moves in a sideways kick that knocks Fiona's legs out from under her and slams her to the ground. She hits hard.

The only thing I hear from her is a groan as she curls up in pain.

"Seymour Rice's research has been online for close to an hour, along with a video Carly took of you showing her how to kill me. Prison for safety, Fiona."

I stand, and I run faster than I ever have in my life.

32

We Confuse a Judge

Four Months and a Few Days Later

"Nice run today, Meadows!" Coach Claus yells from the other side of the track. "Don't forget to bring your A-game for the meet on Saturday! I'm not going to run it for you!"

"I wouldn't want you to," I mumble, not loud enough for him to hear.

I don't need him to run it for me. I'm faster now than I ever was in my old Nessa body. I just needed a reason to run faster. Before the accident, I ran fast because I loved it. But after the accident, I didn't know who 'me' was. Now I have lots of people to run for. To prove it, I run as fast as I can to Mom's car parked on the other side of the fence, waiting to pick me up.

"You're sure you want to do this?" Twin asks me in the backseat as I climb in next to her.

"Yes. I've told you like eight million times already." I run the brush through my curly red hair one more time. It's grown out some and is past my shoulders now.

"I don't know — courthouses always make me nervous," she says.

"It needs to be official. I need it to be official. *We* need it to be official."

"Ewwww, can you stop? You know it creeps me out when you talk like there are two of you." Twin shakes and twists her body like a giant spider just crawled up the back of her neck.

"Sorry, habit. Look, there's Jaz!"

Mom's car has pulled up in front of the courthouse. I climb out and run over to where Luis is pushing her wheelchair. She's got it all decked out with turquoise glitter tape. It sparkles so much in the bright sun it almost blinds me and I hold my hand up to shield my eyes. Jaz said she still needs her blue.

She hasn't worn her wig since she started taking the Rice medication. It works slower than L.E.A.M. did, but better. Jaz is no longer one of the 0%. The doctors are sure that in a few more weeks her Lupus will be gone. She was on the list for BioMed's first trial thanks to Mr. O'Riley getting her on it. Her hair covers her head with dark, thick curls and is beautiful. And as she says, 'the best part is that it doesn't fall off when I run my fingers through it'.

"I think I saw everyone else go inside already," Jaz says. "Take my arm?"

Twin and Mom have joined us so I link my right arm in her left and Twin links her left arm in Jaz's right so we can help her walk in. Her muscles are still weak, but the doctors say that will come back eventually, too. Just like her hair. Jaz was pretty bad off, so it's taking longer. Luis folds her wheelchair and carries it behind us.

It's a beautiful fall day and the warm breeze blows leaves across the sidewalk, swirling them around us.

"Wait a second." We're in front of the doors when I remember. "Mom? Will you take a picture of us? My camera's in the bag."

"Sure." Mom reaches down into the bag she's carrying for me and pulls out Alexis's camera. She takes a few steps back while we turn around to face the street. We smile when she asks us to.

I want to remember this day for the rest of my life.

Everyone's waiting for us in the giant lobby. I've never been in here before. The ceiling is a few stories high and the outside walls are all windows, bathing us all in a bronze afternoon light.

I hug Cole and Toby, then Mr. and Mrs. O'Riley. Toby even brought Meg with him but she still has a scowl on her face. Maybe that's just how her face looks.

"Wait, I have a present." I dig into the bag Mom carries for me and pull out a flat, wrapped gift with a bow on top. I hand it to Mrs. O'Riley.

"But this is your day," she says.

I shake my head. "It's our day. Mr. O'Riley, when you gave me Alexis's camera I found these photos on it, she took them right before her allergy attack. I'm pretty sure she took them for you."

Alexis's mom unwraps the horribly wrapped box and pulls out three framed photos, the ones of Alexis and her message in the order she meant for it to read.

Whatever happens, it's OK. I love you.

"I never thought to look at what was on the camera before I gave it to you," Alexis's dad says. "Thank you."

At least he can talk. Her mom's a crying mess.

Mr. O'Riley, whose first name is Gordon, fired Fiona Gray immediately. Hopefully one of her prison guards let her know. Thankfully the hospital had already cashed Fiona's huge check for the technology center. They plan to name the center after Alexis.

L.E.A.M. production was put to an immediate halt and BioMed's scientists set to work making a viable product with Seymour's research. As did about ten other companies. They compete against each other which helps keep the cost low. Jaz got worse before there was a version BioMed felt safe enough to give her, which is why it's taking her longer to recover. I like to call it the 'Lion Tamer Miracle' — I think Luis had a lot more to do with it than I did.

Mary Rice sends me a thank you card with a sardine pie each month. I opened the first few, not realizing what they were. But now I know the shape of the box and just dump it straight into the trash when it arrives. I'm sure vitamin B12 is great for my body, but I'm not stupid enough to get it that way.

I have the print of Alexis holding the 'It's OK' sign hanging on the wall of my bedroom. I know it wasn't meant for me, and the other two photos didn't apply since Alexis didn't even know me before she died. But when things get hard dealing with the her-thing, the me-thing, and the us-thing I like to look at it. It's kind of comforting to think she knows I'm doing the best I can with this body she's given me.

"I just checked at the front desk," Mom says, rejoining us. "You're supposed to report to Probate Courtroom #5 on the tenth floor in five minutes. We'd better get moving."

It's a good thing the elevators are good-sized. Ten of us and a folded wheelchair squeeze inside and ride up until the little light flashes the number ten and the door opens.

At least Mom thought to bring me some nice clothes; a black and green striped skirt and a matching green button-down shirt that I threw on over my track clothes in the car on the way here. I even changed out of my sneakers which hardly *ever* happens. Because you never know when you're going to have to dive out of a mangled car and run from guys in suits with guns and a fake doctor with leopard-printed heels that could kill you in a back alley.

My nerves kick into high gear when the double doors to the courtroom open. So much for the nice clothes. They're going to be dripping with sweat in about thirty seconds. Cole reaches over and squeezes my hand but it's so clammy it just kind of slides right out of his grip.

When they call my name, I take slow, deliberate steps to the front so I don't trip. I keep my back straight so I look older than I feel right now.

The judge is a bald man with glasses that fall to the tip of his nose when he looks at the stack of papers in front of him.

"Vanessa Meadows. I have an application here for a name change. This is a pretty unusual request. Why are you requesting to legally add 'Alexis' as your middle name?"

I've practiced my answer for weeks, to the point where I could recite it as well as The Pledge of Allegiance. But now, in front of this strange man, my mind is blank.

"Your honor," I begin because those are the only two words of my memorized response that comes to me. I close my eyes and let the rest of the words come out. From where I don't know.

"I lost my body in a car accident almost a year and a half ago. Doctors took my brain and transplanted it into Alexis O'Riley's body, who lost her life the day before. At first, I hated her body. It was everything that my old body wasn't. Then I got to know Alexis and her family and friends and realize that she's as much a part of me now as

I'm a part of her. My parents never gave me a middle name when I was born and I think it was kismet. They didn't give me a middle name so I could someday use hers." And now I know where the words came from. They came from my heart, not my mind. They came from *our* heart.

Jaz hands me a tissue and I rub it across my face furiously.

The judge takes a breath that sounds like a giant sigh.

"And I thought your name-change request was odd." He takes a big stamp, inks it on a pad, and pounds it onto the top sheet on his stack.

"Congratulations. You are now legally Vanessa Alexis Meadows."

Yes. Yes, I am.

A Note From the Author

I've spent a lot of years in a body that has been trying to kill me — or at least make my life a lot more difficult. I was born with a disease called Charcot Marie Tooth disease (or CMT) and some days I do feel like this body is trying to do me in. It hasn't been easy — especially when I was in school and kids would make fun of how I walk or laugh when I fell, which was pretty much every day.

But if a genie appeared in front of me and asked me for a wish (or even 3!) I wouldn't wish for a new body. It's taken some time, but this body and I have been through a lot together and I love it now. It's taught me compassion and empathy and how to look through someone's exterior and see the amazing person they are on the inside.

Whatever happens, it's OK. I love you.

No matter what body you happen to be in today.

Acknowledgements

Chad — thank you for always understanding when your wife just needs to create, and for helping me brainstorm whenever I need ideas. Thank you for being my best friend and my soul mate. I love you. Audrey and Natalie — my two reasons for everything. You both fill me with so much love and pride — being your mom is my very favorite thing.

Renee Kunkel and Karen Redfearn — thank you for being the perfect writing partners, for inspiring me and keeping me writing. And thanks to the North Central Ohio Writers group, especially Carma Shoemaker, for always giving us a place to write and a fun and friendly environment to do it in. Hey - if we can write in a convent, we can write *anywhere*! And the Get Lit! book club — Diedre Policz & Renee — for always keeping me reading.

To ALEXIS's early critique and beta readers — Debbi Broderick, Christa Brubaker, Kristy Boyce, Robin Hall, Larry Kaufman, Tara Kuczykowski, Diane Majewski, Dee Romito, Abby Sendelbach, Deb Spreng, Kimberly VanderHorst, Gordi Wendling and Beth Zody — I can't thank you enough for reading and helping me bring this story to life (especially those hearts, Abby). And my niece Jocelyn Van Dyne, who is already such an amazing writer — thank you for reading and I can't wait to read the many books that you write!

And to all of my St. Mary's students over the past twelve years — you all have inspired me in countless ways, even when you didn't realize you were.
Keep reading!

About the Author

Holly VanDyne is the author of books for both children and teens. *The Inhabitant of Alexis O'Riley* is her first published novel. She is a librarian, art and STEM teacher at a small K-8 school, a lover of LEGO's and stickers, and lives in Mansfield, Ohio with her husband, two daughters, and two dogs.

You can learn more about her and
the books she writes at
http://www.hollyvandyne.com

Made in the USA
Las Vegas, NV
19 August 2021